Praise for Kevin Barry's

Beatlebone

"Extraordinary.... Kevin Barry's *Beatlebone* is a strange, intense and slightly incoherent extended fantasy.... [Barry's] super-charged prose style ... borrows heavily from James Joyce, Flann O'Brien, J. P. Donleavy and other past masters of extravagant Irish lyricism at its high-modernist peak."   —*The Washington Post*

"Barry has a wry, pitch-perfect ear for dialogue and an equally affecting eye for character traits."
                    —*San Francisco Chronicle*

"*Beatlebone*, the novel, reads as brilliant liner notes for a nervous breakdown, a hip, alternative history for Lennon's lost years."   —NPR

"There's music to Barry's prose: Smart rhythms dart through his sentences; taut bridges join his paragraphs.... His dialogue is whimsical, sometimes hilarious, catching the idiom of the local life, and, in *Beatlebone*, nailing John Lennon, the wittiest and darkest Beatle, spot on."   —*Slate*

"This glorious lark feels canonical."
                    —*New York* magazine

"*Beatlebone* is an odyssey of the mind. Its ever-shifting modes vividly recall James Joyce's *Ulysses*. . . . The island simply represents an idea. What's at stake in his getting to the island? We never really know, which is a tricky feat to pull off. Barry succeeds by parsing John's limbo state so clearly and vividly."

—*Minneapolis Star Tribune*

"Nearly every sentence exhibits the care and craft of a poet. Barry doesn't waste a word."   —*The A.V. Club*

"It's a musical fever dream of a book that sounds weirder than it is; Barry's perfectly honed storytelling voice sweeps readers happily through decades and across rough seas."   —*BookPage*

"Barry's prose is at once dreamy and direct, ethereal and grounded."   —*Paste*

"*Beatlebone* is a perfect novel for someone who loves good fiction, or who wants to dive into the human condition, or any Beatles fan."   —*The Kansas City Star*

" 'The examined life turns out to be a pain in the stones,' Lennon says near the end of *Beatlebone*. But Barry's keenly worded quest is worth the trip."

—*Las Vegas Weekly*

Kevin Barry

Beatlebone

Kevin Barry is the author of the highly acclaimed novel *City of Bohane* and two short-story collections, *Dark Lies the Island* and *There Are Little Kingdoms*. He was awarded the Rooney Prize in 2007 and won the Sunday Times EFG Short Story Award in 2012. For *City of Bohane*, he was shortlisted for the Costa First Novel Award and the Irish Book Award, and won the Authors' Club Best First Novel Award, the European Union Prize for Literature, and the IMPAC Dublin Literary Award. His short fiction has appeared in *The New Yorker* and elsewhere. He lives in County Sligo in Ireland.

Beatlebone

Beatlebone

A NOVEL

KEVIN BARRY

Anchor Books
A Division of Penguin Random House LLC
New York

FIRST ANCHOR BOOKS EDITION, OCTOBER 2016

Copyright © 2015 by Kevin Barry

All rights reserved. Published in the United States by Anchor Books,
a division of Penguin Random House LLC, New York. Originally
published in hardcover in Great Britain by Canongate Books Ltd.,
in 2015, and in the United States by Doubleday, a division of
Penguin Random House LLC, New York, in 2015.

Anchor Books and colophon are registered trademarks of
Penguin Random House LLC.

The Library of Congress has cataloged the Doubleday edition
as follows:
Beatlebone / Kevin Barry. —First edition.
Pages ; cm
I. Lennon, John, 1940–1980—Fiction.   2. Psychological fiction.
I. Title.
PR6102.A7833B43 2015
823'.92—dc23
2015035098

Anchor Books Trade Paperback ISBN: 978-1-101-91133-4
eBook ISBN: 978-0-385-54030-8

Book design by Michael Collica

www.anchorbooks.com

Printed in the United States of America
10 9 8 7 6 5 4 3 2 1

For Eugene, Joan, Majella, Mary

. . . the most elusive island of all, the first person singular.

—*John McGahern*

Contents

Beatlebone

Part One

JOHN MOVES BY ENGINE OF MELANCHOLY—1978

He sets out for the place as an animal might, as though on some fated migration. There is nothing rational about it nor even entirely sane and this is the great attraction. He's been travelling half the night east and nobody has seen him—if you keep your eyes down, they can't see you. Across the strung-out skies and through the eerie airports and now he sits in the back of the old Mercedes. His brain feels like a city centre and there is a strange tingling in the bones of his monkey feet. Fuck it. He will deal with it. The road unfurls as a black tongue and laps at the night. There's something monkeyish, isn't there, about his feet? Also his gums are bleeding. But he won't worry about that now—he'll worry about it in a bit. Save one for later. Trees and fields pass by in the grainy night. Monkeys on the fucking brain lately as a matter of fact. Anxiety? He hears a blue yonderly note from somewhere, perhaps it's from within. Now the driver's sombre eyes show up in the rearview—

It's arranged, he says. There should be no bother whatsoever. But we could be talking an hour yet to the hotel out there?

Driver has a very smooth timbre, deep and trustworthy like a newscaster, the bass note and brown velvet of his voice, or the corduroy of it, and the great chunky old Merc cuts the air quiet as money as they move.

John is tired but not for sleeping.

No fucking pressmen, he says. And no fucking photogs.

In the near dark there is the sense of trees and fields and hills combining. The way that you can feel a world form around you on a lucky night in the springtime. He rolls the window an inch. He takes a lungful of cool starlight for a straightener. Blue and gasses. That's lovely. He is tired as fuck but he cannot get his head down. It's the Maytime—the air is thick with and tastes of it—and he's all stirred up again.

Where the fuck are we, driver?

It'd be very hard to say.

He quite likes this driver. He stretches out his monkey toes. It's the middle of the night and fucking nowhere. He sighs heavily—this starts out well enough but it turns quickly to a dull moaning. Not a handsome development. Driver's up the rearview again. As though to say *gather yourself*. For a moment they watch each other gravely; the night moves. The driver has a high purple colour—madness or eczema—and his nose looks dead and he speaks now in a scolding hush:

That's going to get you nowhere.

Driver tips the wheel, a soft glance; the road is turned. They are moving fast and west. Mountains climb the night sky. The cold stars travel. They are getting higher. The air changes all the while. By a scatter of woods there is a medieval scent. By a deserted house on a sudden turn there is an occult air. How to explain these fucking things? They come at last by the black gleaming sea and this place is so haunted

or at least it is for me

and there is a sadness, too, close in, like a damp and second skin. Out here the trees have been twisted and shaped by the wind into strange new guises—he can see witches, ghouls, creatures-of-nightwood, pouting banshees, cackling hoods.

It's a night for the fucking bats, he says.

I beg your pardon?

What I mean to say is I'm going off my fucking bean back here.

I'm sorry?

That's all you can be.

He lies back in his seat, pale and wakeful, chalk-white come-dian; his sore bones and age. No peace, no sleep, no meaning. And the sea is out there and moving. He hears it drag on its cables—a slow, rusted swooning. Which is poetical, to a man in the dark hours, in his denim, and lonely—it moves him.

Driver turns, smiling sadly—

You've the look of a poor fella who's caught up in himself.

Oh?

What's it's on your mind?

Not easy to say.

Love, blood, fate, death, sex, the void, mother, father, cunt and prick—these are the things on his mind.

Also—

How many more times are they going to ask me to come on The *fucking* Muppet Show?

I just want to get to my island, he says.

He will spend three days alone on his island. That is all that he asks. That he might scream his fucking lungs out and scream the days into nights and scream to the stars by night—if stars there are and the stars come through.

———

The moon browses the fields and onwards through the night they move—the moon is up over the fields and trees for bad-ness' sake but he cannot even raise a howl.

Radio?

Go on then.

Will we chance a bit of Luxembourg?

Yeah, let's try a little Luxy.

But they are playing Kate Bush away on her wiley, windy fucking moors.

Question, he says.

Yes?

What the fuck is wiley?

Does she not say winding?

She says wiley.

Well . . .

Turn it off, he says.

Witchy fucking screeching. The hills fall away and the dark-ness tumbles. Now in the distance a town is held in the palm of its own lights—a little kingdom there—and after a long, vague while—he is breathing but not much alive—they come to an old bridge and he asks to stop a moment by the river and have a listen.

Here?

Yeah, just here.

It's four in the morning—the motor idles at a low hum—and the trees have voices, and the river has voices, and they are very old.

Driver turns—

Hotel's the far side of the town just another few miles.

But John looks outside and he listens very hard and he settles to his course.

You can leave me here, he says.

———

He planned to live out on his island for a bit but he never did. He bought it when he was twenty-seven in the middle of a dream. But now it's the Maytime again and he's come over a bit strange and dippy again—the hatches to the underworld are opening—and he needs to sit on his island again just for a short while and alone and look out on the bay and the fat knuckle of the holy mountain across the bay and have a natter with the bunnies and get down with the starfish and lick the salt off his chops and waggle his head like a dog after rain and Scream and let nobody come find him.

The black Mercedes sits idling and lit by the bridge that spans the talking river.

John walks from the car in a slow measured reverse—one foot backwards and then the other.

He is so many miles from love now and home.

This is the story of his strangest trip.

―――――

And the season is at its hinge. The moment soon will drop its weight to summer. The river is a rush of voices over its ruts and tunnels into the soft black flesh of the night and woods, and the driver leans at rest against the bonnet of the car— casually, unworried, his arms folded, if anything amused— and as the door is open, the car is lit against the dark and the stonework of the old bridge and the small town that rises beyond by its chimney pots and vaulting gables. John steps another foot back, and another, and he laughs aloud but not snidely—the driver is getting smaller; still he watches amusedly—and the town and the river and bridge and the Mercedes by stepped degrees recede and became smaller

what if I keep going without seeing where I'm going
what if I keep going into the last of the night and trees

and he steps off the road and into a ditch and his footing gives and he stumbles and falls onto his backside and into the black cold shock of ditchwater. He laughs again and rights himself and he turns now and walks into the field and quickens.

He does not answer to his name as it calls across the night and air.

———

It is such a clear night and warm. He walks into the fields until he is a good distance from the road. He can speak her name across the sky. Feel its lights again in his mouth. Fucking hell. He is so weary, and fucked, and Scouse—a sentimentalist. The ground's soft give beneath his feet is luxurious. He wants to lie down into the soft rich cake of it and does. It is everything that he needs. He turns onto his belly and lies facedown in the dirt and digs his nails in hard—

Cling the fuck on, John.

The sphere of the night turns by its tiny increments. The last of the night swings across its arches and greys. He can do anything he wants to do. He can live in a Spanish castle; he can run with the tides of the moon. He turns his face to settle his cheek on the dirt. He rests for a while. Mars is a dull fire in the eastern sky. He lies for a long calm while until the hills are woken and the birds come to flirt and call and he feels clairvoyant now and newly made.

John lies saddled on the warm earth and he listens to its bones.

———

He's been coming loose of himself since early in the spring. He knows all the signs of it. One minute he's lost in the past and the next he's shot back to the now. There is no future in it. The year is on the turn and greening and everything is too fucking alive again.

And he has been haunted by his own self for such a long while, he has been endlessly fascinated by his own black self this long while—he is aching, he is godhead, he is a right bloody monster—but now he is thirty-seven—

I mean thirty fucking seven?

—and he wants at last to be over himself—he's all grown— and he looks out and into the world and he can see it clearly and true for the kip it is and the shithole it is and the sweet heaven—the mons—of love and sex and sleep it is, or can be, and he is scabrous (there's a word) and tender—he is both—and there's a whole wealth of fucking motherlove— even still—being the sentimental Scouse—her death's gleam his dark star—and the old town that was coal-black and majestic—wasn't it?—or at least on its day and the way it was giddy by its night—alewaft and fagsmoke, peel of church bell—and a rut down an alleyway—wasn't there?—midnight by church bell, cuntsmell—

oh my sweet my paleskin my soft-lipped girlie

—and now he's got a throb on, and he's coming down Bold Street, and it's the city of Liverpool, and he's seventeen years old, and he's a North-of-England honky with spud-Irish blood and that is what he is and that is all that he is and inside him, deep down—*listen*—the way the drunken notes stir.

———

He sits up in the field. He looks around himself warily. Jesus fuck. He sits in the raw grey light and the cold damp air. He has inarguably placed himself in fucking Ireland again. He has a think about this and he has a fag. A whip of cold wind comes across the field and the tall grasses flex and sway—he sneezes. They say that your soul stops, don't they? Or at least fucks off for a bit. He stands up for a coughing fit. His poor lungs, those tired soldiers. He proceeds on walkabout. Listen for a song beneath the skin of the earth. Seeing as he cannot fucking find one elsewhere. He aims back for the road again. Panicky, yes, but you just keep on walking. And maybe in this way, John, you can leave the past behind.

———

He finds his own trace back through the long grass. He crosses the bridge in wet light. A sombre friend, a heron, stands greyly and still and what's-the-fucking-word by the edge of the river and town. He walks on up the town. Sentinel is the word. His words are fucked and all over. Weeks of half-sleep. Weeks of night sweats and hilarity. Except this time with no fucking songs in tow. The little town is deserted as a wartime beach. He sits down on a bench in the empty square. Have a breather, Missus Alderton. He has a look around. Okay. He must look like one half of a Pete-and-Dudley routine. Why exactly is he here in this nothing town in this nowhere place and on the wrong side of the ocean and so far from those that he loves and home? Maybe he knows that out here he can be alone.

It's the earliest of the morning and still but for the leaves. He walks the edges of the square under the moving leaves. He goes by the sleeping grocery and the sleeping church and there's a smug little infirmary, too—he thinks, that'll be me. His empathy—to be old and sick, how would that be? Stout matron smells of talc and jam tarts. A last shimmer in the throb department? Ah but forlornly, yes. Okay. Move along, John. Keep it fucking cheerful, let's. Random words appear on his lips as he walks the few and empty streets of the early morning town. Here's a new entry—woebegone. But that's quite lovely, actually. He doubles back to the square again. Senses a half-movement down below: the heron, as it turns its regal clockwork head to watch him now from its place by the river. Bead of eye from one to the other. News for me, at all? Nothing good, I expect. The metallic gleam of its grey coat in the cold sun. Otherworldly, the sense of it—something alien there. Walk the fuck on again. He sees a fat old dog having a snooze down a sideway. Ah sweetness. He watches for a moment and he gets a bit teary, in fact, about the juddery little sighs of the dog's breathing—he is out in the world now—and his fat sleeping belly and he can see his doggy dreams of bones and cats and flirty poodles smoking Gitanes and perking their high tight poodle asses in the air.

The air is thick and salty. You could bite a chunk off. Sniff out the sea-bite's hint-of-vulva, John, mummy-smell. He has a tricky five minutes but he comes through. He turns up a display board for tourists. The board has a map on and now all the names from nine years past—his last visit—come rattling again. Newport, Mulranny, Achill Island and there's the great jaggedy bay, Clew Bay, with all its tiny islands. There are tens and dozens and hundreds of these islands. He reads that there are three hundred and sixty-five islands all told; there is an island for every day of the fucking year—

So how will he tell which island is his?

There are rustles and movements. He is alone but not—he can hear the shifting of the town ghosts. Clocking off from the night shift. He blinks three times to make those fuckers disappear. He has his ritual things. He has a fag and listens. He inhales deep, holds it, and his heart thumps; he exhales slow. He wants to make a connection with you now. He is thirty-seven years along the road—the slow-quick, slow-quick road—and he lives in a great fortress high above the plain where the fearsome injuns roam—those bold Manhattoes—and now if he whispers it, very very softly—a particular word—and if you listen for it—very very carefully—

Do you think you can hear him still?

———

The fat old dog moseys out from the sideway. There is evidence here of great male bewilderment. It's in the poor bugger's walk; it's in his carry. He looks down the length of the town and shakes his head against it. He looks on up the town—the same. He does not appear to notice yet the presence of a stranger. He sniffs at the gutter—it's not good. He has a long, slow rub off the grocer's wall—it's still there, and the pebbledash gets at the awkward bits nicely. He edges onto the square on morning patrol but he's hassled-looking, weary, and the fleshy haunches roll slowly as he goes. He stops up in the middle of the square, now in a devout or philosophical hold, as the breeze brings news to twitch the bristles of his snout, and he growls halfheartedly, and turns to find the line of scent and a tatty man in denims on the bench.

Good morning, John says.

The dog raises an eye in wariness—he is careful, an old-stager. He comes across but cautiously and he looks soul-deep into John's eyes and groans.

I know exactly how you feel, John says.

And now the fat old dog rests its chin on his knee, and he places a palm on the breathing warmth of the dog's flank, and they share a moment's sighing grace.

Never name the moment for happiness or it will pass by.

The dog lies down to settle by his feet and sets a drooly chin on the toe of a fresh purple sneaker.

Those are not long from the bloody box, John says.

He reaches down and lifts the dog's chin with a finger and he finds such a sweet sadness there and a very particular handsomeness, a kind of gooey handsomeness, and at once he names the dog—

Brian Wilson, he says.

At which the dog wags a weary tail, and apparently grins, and John laughs now and he begins to sing a bit in high pitch—

Well it's been building up inside of me
For oh, I don't know how long . . .

The dog comes in to moan softly and tunefully, in perfect counterpoint to him—this morning's duet—and John is thinking:

This escapade is getting out of hand right off the fucking bat.

————

A brown car rolls slowly from the top of the town. John and the dog Brian Wilson turn their snouts and beady eyes to inspect. The car has a tiny pea-headed chap inside for a driver. He's barely got his eyes over the top of the wheel. He stalls by the grocer's but he keeps the engine running. He steps out of the juddering car. There is something jockey-like or Aintree-week about this tiny, wiry chap. He fetches a bundle of newspapers from the backseat of the car and carries them to the stoop of the grocer's.

Well? he says.

Well enough, John says.

He places the bundle on the stoop and takes a penknife from his arse pocket and cuts the string on the bundle and pulls the top paper free and he has a quick read, the engine all the while breathing, and Brian Wilson scowling, and John sits huddled against the morning chill that moves across the town in sharp points from the river.

I'll tell you one thing for nothin', the jockey-type says.

Go on?

This place is run by a pack of fucken apes.

Who're you telling?

He sighs and returns the paper neatly to its bundle. He edges back to the verge of the pavement and looks to a window above the grocery.

No sign of Martin? he says.

And he shakes his head in soft despair—

The misfortune's after putting down a night of it, I'd say.

And with that he is on his way again.

John and the dog Brian Wilson watch him go.

You can never trust a jockey-type, John says, on account of they've got oddly set eyes.

————

A broad-shouldered kid comes walking through the square with an orange football under his arm. As he walks he scans one way and then the other, east and west. The kid has a dead hard face on. As if he's about to invade Russia.

Morning, John says.

Well, the kid says.

The kid stops up and drops the ball and traps it under his foot—he rolls it back and forth in slow pensive consideration.

You one of the Connellans? he says.

I could be, John says.

Ye over for the summer or only a small while?

We'll see how it goes.

Ah yeah.

The kid kicks the ball against the grocer's wall and traps it again and kicks it once more for the rebound.

How's the grandmother keeping?

Not so hot, John says.

She's gone old, of course, the kid says, and winces.

And what age are you now?

I'm ten, he says.

Bloody hell, John says, time's moving.

Could be the brother you're thinking of, the kid says. The brother's Keith. He's only seven yet.

I have you now.

The kid moves on, curtly, with a wave, and kicks the ball as he goes in diagonals to his path, now quickening, now slowing to meet its return and tapping rhyme as it follows the fall-away of the street, an awkward-looking, a bandy-footed kid whose name never will be sung from the heaving terraces— and so the silver river flows.

And the kid crosses the river and walks on and the heron takes off on slow heavy beat-steady wings and the kid's away into the playing fields and the rising morning. It's the sort of thing that could break your heart if you were of a certain type or turn of mind.

If you were a gentleman quick to tears, John says.

And Brian Wilson moans softly again and stretches and yowls in the morning sun.

———

Here's an old lady a-squint behind the wheel of a fab pink Mini as it grumbles and stalls again by the grocer's—centre of the universe, apparently. She wears a knit hat of tangerine shade and a pair of great chunky specs. She rolls the window and sends a pessimistic glance from the milk-bottle lenses.

There is no sign of Martin, I suppose?

He's after a night of it, John says.

She has a German-type accent—the careful inspection of the words as they tip out.

Well that is me fucked and hitting for Westport so, she says.

She takes off again.

———

A lovely old tractor spins from its wheels a dust of dried mud and shite and there's an ancient farmer with a stoved-in face and electrified eyes of bird's-egg blue and he stalls also for a moment and calls down and not a little sternly—

Cornelius O'Grady is lookin' for you.

And he moves on again and the old dog rises from his feet and coughs up a forlorn bark and heads back to the sideway.

More fun in it asleep than awake, John says.

He has a look about. There's that small hotel at the top of the square. It sits there with an air of grim inevitability. He shrugs and rises—

I mean what's the very worst that could happen?

———

Reception is deserted but they're banging pots and pans together out the back. A demented brass band. Morning engagements only. He smells the green of bacon being fried up. Wallow in the waft of grease and smoke. Eat the pig and act the goat. He presses the bell. Nobody shows. He presses again and waits. There's no rush on. He presses again and a hatchet-faced crone appears on the tip of her witch's snout. Looks him up and down. Sour as the other Monday's milk. Double-checks his ankles to see if he's got a suitcase hid down there.

Well? she says.

It's about a room, love.

She throws an eye up the clock.

This is a foxy hour to be landing into a hotel, she says.

And in denim, he says.

The reception's air is old and heavy, as in a sickroom's, and the clock swings through its gloomy moments.

Do you have a reservation? she says.

I have severe ones, he says, but I do need a room.

She sucks her teeth. She opens a ledger. She raises her eye-glasses. She has a good long read of her ledger.

Does it say anything in there about a room, love?

She searches out her mouth with the tip of a green tongue.

It's about a room? he says.

With great and noble sorrow she turns and from a hook on a wooden rack takes down a key—he feels like he's been hanging from that rack for years.

The best room you can do me?

They don't differ much, she says, and switches the key for another—he'll get the worse for asking.

Payment in advance, she says.

No surprise there.

Name? she says, and he rustles one from the air.

She leads him up a stair that smells of mouse and yesteryear and they climb again to an attic floor and the eaves lean in as if they could tell a few secrets—hello?—and at the end of a dark passage they come to a scary old wooden door.

Is this where you keep the hunchback? he says.

She scowls and slides the key and turns its oily clicks.

He thanks her as he squeezes by—hello?—and for half a moment she brightens. She lays a papery hand on his— quality of mothskin; the veins ripped like junkie veins—and she whispers—

Your man? she says. You're very like him.

Not as much as I used to be, he says.

———

He started to Scream with Dr. Janov in California. He was worked up one-on-one. He was worked up fucking hard. He sat there for hours, and for months, and he went deep. He wasn't for holding back. He hollered and he ranted and he Screamed. He cursed everybody, he cursed them all, he cursed the blood. Dr. Janov said he needed to get at the blood—he went at the blood.

Mother, father.

Cunt and prick.

What had stirred and made and deformed him. What had down all the years deranged him. He was angry as hell. They worked together four months out on the coast. Dr. Janov wore a crown of beautiful white curls—it shimmered in the sun. Dr. Janov spoke of amorphous doom and nameless dread and the hurt brain. It was no fucking picnic out on the coast. He squatted on the terrace and he looked out to the sea and he was heartsore and he drank fucking orange juice and he wept until he was weak. He had a shadow beneath the skin and he was so very fucking weak.

Dr. Janov said that fame was a scouring and a hollow thing—he said there's fucking news. Dr. Janov said he should ignore it—he said you fucking try. Dr. Janov said he should channel his anger and not smoke pot—he said I'll see what I can do.

Dr. Janov said he should Scream, and often, and he saw at once an island in his mind.

Windfucked, seabeaten.

The west of Ireland—the place of the old blood.

A place to Scream.

———

He sits in his tomb up top of the Newport hotel. It contains a crunchy armchair, a floppy bed, several arrogant spiders, a mattress with stains the shapes of planets and an existential crisis. But he wouldn't want to sound too French about it.

He looks out the window. It really is a very pretty day. The street runs down to the river, and there is the bridge across, and the hills rising and

lah-de-dah,
lah-de-dum-dum dah

the green, the brown, the treetops, and it means nothing to him at all. Across the square a flash of hard light, turning—a swallow's belly, and now dark again, and his mind flips and turns in just that same way. He wants to get to his island but unseen and unheard of—he wants to be no more than a rustle, no more than a shade.

He makes the calls that he needs to make. It's arranged that a fixer will be sent the next day. He lies on the bed for a while but cannot sleep. He takes his clothes off and climbs from the bed. He has a bit of a turn. He scrunches up in the arm-chair by the window. He's all angles and edges. He speaks aloud and for a long while. He speaks to his love—his eyes close—and he speaks to his mother. Fucking hell. The hours he spends in the chair are like years—

He is a boy.
He is a man.
He is a very very old man.

—and he sits all day until the sun has gone around the building and the room is almost dark again. A day that feels slow as a century—he might be out there still. The evening gets chilly and he climbs onto the bed. He wraps himself in a blanket and phones downstairs. He has a long Socratic debate that after a certain period of time results in a bowl of brown vegetable soup arriving. The kid that brings it has a perfectly ovaline face on as flat as a penny.

You'd be quicker on roller skates, John says.

He slurps down the soup. He sits wrapped in his blanket. The soup is that hot it makes him cross-eyed. The bed is moving about like a sea. A call comes in from the fixer. Something deep and familiar to the voice—like a newscaster, and he sees the high purple face again, the dead nose, the fattish driver.

You again?

Well.

He is asked gently of his needs. It's as if he's had a loss. He is on a bloody raft the way the bed is moving about.

The important thing, again, he says, is no newspapers, no reporters, no TV.

Not easy.

Another thing, he says. I can't remember exactly where the island is.

Okey-doke.

But I do know its name.

Well that's a start.

The arrangement is made—they will set off first thing.

What was your name anyhow?

My name is Cornelius O'Grady.

Cornelius?

———

The way that age comes and goes in a life—he'll never be as old again as he was when he was twenty-seven. In the attic room at the small hotel he paces and laughs and the words come in pattern for a bit but they will not hold. No, they will not fucking hold. He looks out to the town square by night. It is deserted but not static—it comes and goes in time and the breeze. Half the time, in this life, you wouldn't know where you are nor when. There are moments of unpleasant liveliness. Tamp that the fuck down is best. He aims for the telephone. He builds himself up to it. He breathes deep and dials and there is a transaction of Arabic intrigue with the fucking desk down there. It works out, eventually—the roller-skate kid fetches a glass of whiskey up.

That'll put hairs on me chest, he says.

Okay, the kid says.

Peat and smoke—it tastes of the past and uncles, sip by the beaded sip. He doesn't really drink anymore. No booze, no junk, no blow. These are the fucking rules. He is macrobiotic. He is brown-rice-and-vegetables. The stations of the fucking cross. A read—that would be an idea. The room has grown sombre as the night finds its depth. What's the fucking word? Crepuscular. He flicks a lamp switch against it. The amber light of the lamp as it warms weakly on the old flock wallpaper brings the waft or flavour—you can't miss it—of Edwardian time. Oh and here's a word—Edwardiana. Very nice. The word gives dapperness, and tapered strides, and teddy boys. He looks around his tiny room beneath the eaves and laughs—the West of Ireland by night. Oh just taking the fucking air, really. I'll have a stroll in a bit. Try not to fuck myself in the briney. Fathomless depths, et cetera. Oh Christ, a read—fill up this sour brain with words. He slides a drawer on the tiny dresser—the dresser is so tiny it might be for the fittings of elves—and there is no Gideon's, not as such, but there is an old book there:

The Anatomy of Melancholy by Richard Burton

Richard fucking Burton? What kind of establishment is this? Now the melodious syllables come to shape his lips— hammy, taffy, lispy, vaguely faggy? How did it go? In *Under Milk Wood*? He looks in the dull silver of the dresser's mirror and mouths the words—

I know there are
Towns lovelier than ours,
And fairer hills and loftier far,
And groves more full of flowers
And boskier woods more blithe with spring . . .

Boskier? Fuck me. He flicks through the pages. Okay. It's a different Richard. And there are all sorts herein. He falls onto the bed. He unknits his long, cold limbs. He falls into the drugged pages. He reads for hours and every now and then

Thou canst not think worse of me than I do of myself.

he speaks aloud but

Melancholy can be overcome only by melancholy.

just the two words, repeated

He that increaseth wisdom, increaseth sorrow.

over and over again

If you like not my writing, go read something else.

fuck me,
fuck me,
fuck me.

———

At last he gives in to the night or at least makes an arrangement with it. He sleeps a long, unquiet sleep disturbed by
quick dreams of woodland places. These come as no great
surprise. He meets elves and sprites and clowning devils.
Anxiety? He wakes at last to a new world and to a morning
lost in a heavy mist. Sorely his bones ache—he traces the
length of the soreness with a long, dull, luxurious sighing.
Which is very pleasant, as it happens. Though also he feels
about ninety fucking six. The grey buildings outside have
softened in the mist and in places have all but disappeared.
The hills across the river are entirely wiped out. He feels
oddly at home, as though he's woken to this place every day
of his life: a sentimentalist. Maybe as the grocer or as the
farmer or as the priest. Now his calm is broken by a set of
angry steps come along the passage and a mad rapping on
the door and the door is nearly off its bloody hinges—

You'd better come in!

It's Hatchet-Face, his favourite crone, and she's on the war-
path—

Great spouts of steam gush from her hairy ears.

Her pinned eyes are livid and searching.

Her mouth contorts to a twisted O.

Who's dead? he says.

She runs a filthy look around the room.

She sniffs the air as if he's pissed the bed.

Do you realise, she says, that it's hapist ten in the morning?

Hapist? he says. Already?

There are people, she says, with half a day put down.

Best thing you can do with days.

She eyes him—an owl for a mouse—and sucks her teeth. There is dark auntly suspicion in the glance, as if he's been having a sneaky one off the handle. A clamminess, as of families. He has been drawn back into something here. The clock runs backwards. He holds the covers boyishly against his chest.

Had I better make a move, love?

You'd better, she says. There's a woman down there has a home to go to.

A woman?

That does the breakfasts.

Oh, he says. Her with the brass band.

She has the mother bad. The mother is left with half a lung to her name. The other half is not viable. Or so they're saying. All I know is she'd want to be gone home to the mother an hour since or the mother'll be gone out the blasted window. Again.

To be honest, love, I'm not big on brekkie. A Pepsi and a fag'll do me. Mothers out windows?

That wouldn't be the worst of it, she says. But you'd want to come down anyway—I have a Mr. O'Grady waiting on you.

As she says his name, she fixes her hair and works her lips to an unseemly fullness.

He says you've a man here called McCarthy? I says, well! I says I think I have anyhow.

————

Mother Mary of Jesus is sat up the dining room wall, blue and weeping, her long glance so loving—a tear of blood rolls.

Cornelius O'Grady is sat just beneath—his hair is greased and fixed like a ducktail joint.

Would you mind sitting down, John, he says. You're making me dizzy.

Daylight shows Cornelius in high fettle. There is vim and spark and big vitality. He considers John at length and silently; he shakes his head in amused suffering.

The problem, he says, is they'd probably know you alright.

He returns woefully to his breakfasts. He has two fried breakfasts laid out on the white linen. He moves the great boulder of a head in slow swoops over the plates as though by the arm of a crane. He slices daintily into the meats and chews and smiles grimly.

But all we can do is fucken try, he says.

A powerful chewer: the way his massive chin swings side to side and churns—they are handing out the chins around here. He mops a hunk of bread across the yellow of the egg yolks, and there is the smell of burnt fat and greasy cloy.

Have you not et? he says.

I'm fine, Cornelius. I'll have a fag in a bit.

Humorous eyes; a shaking of the head. He zips from plate to plate and back again. He is very neat about his work, slicing a rasher here, a sausage there, having a chew and half a grilled tomato, a soft chuckling, a little sigh of thanks.

Black pudding? John says.

Yes?

Congealed blood is what it is.

You wouldn't eat a bit?

Me? I'm macrobiotic.

Which means you ate what, fleas?

Hatchet-Face comes to work around the edges of the room, tidying and settling away, but really just the better to observe Cornelius and his great handsome bull's head: we are in the presence of legend.

About my situation, Mr. O'Grady?

Yes?

I really don't need a fucking circus right now. The most important thing is no one knows I'm out here.

Cornelius fills his mug from a silver pot and runs his eyes about the room.

John, he says, half the newspapermen in Dublin are after piling onto the Westport train.

Oh for fucksake!

But we aren't beat yet. The train's an hour till it's in. We'll throw a shape lively.

He's bigger sat down than he is stood up. Short-legged, squat, the giant head rolls cockily as they move, and Cornelius aims a wave for Hatchet-Face—she flutters as though for a sexy saint.

All I want is to get to my island.

Which is it is yours?

It's called Dorinish.

You'd say it Durn-ish.

You know the one?

There are maps but I'd pay no mind to them. Wait for me at the back door and I'll swing the van around.

The van?

Is right.

What's happened our Merc?

That wasn't my car at all, John.

And where are we headed exactly?

Cornelius sends up his sighs. He looks at his pale charge sadly, as though at a tiny injured bird, and he jerks a black thumb over his shoulder.

West, he says.

———

The van's a bone-rattler, a money-shaker, all rust and lung disease, and it screeches for death as it revs up pace for the sudden turns and the gut-heaving drops: see now how the land falls away. There is mist on the hills; he can see reaching for the crags and granite tops the wispy fingers of the mist on the hills, and Cornelius's blue eyes are set to a high murderous burn—his hilarity—and John is on the lam and loves it although he has a sad stretch, about home, but just for a half-mile or so—it passes—and the van screams and barks and it smells of the other Monday's fish: John's stomach lurches and his soul groans. He lights another fag, an evil Gitane.

There's one day I'd be after mackerel, Cornelius says. There's another day I'd be dosing sheep. Another again? I'd be playing the chauffeur. And only last Thursday gone? I dug a grave for a man that took a sudden stroke . . . Sixty-two years of age and he only trying to watch a bit of television. God rest him.

Cornelius quickens the van for a blind turn. He accelerates again to come out of the bend. He plays at full volume a vile country music all twangy hoedowns and cry-it-to-the-moon laments but in awful, reaching, sobbing, spud-Irish voices.

John eyeballs the fucker hard—

Cornelius?

—but he is paid no mind.

He slaps eject to pop the cassette but Cornelius slaps it back to play again.

Ray Lynam, he says. That's one powerful fucken singer.

Keep the dogs at bay. This is the most important thing. Keep the hissing pack at bay and get me to my fucking island. His new friend whistles jauntily as he steers the van.

Cornelius?

Yes, John?

You do realise it's extremely fucking important that no one knows I'm out here?

I do of course.

Because it would ruin everything, Cornelius. It would defeat the whole fucking purpose.

I understand, John. But I've a feeling the fuckers aren't far off our trail.

How can you tell?

From the way the air is settling around us.

His eyes shoot to the rearview, to the wings.

Do you understand what I mean by that?

I've no fucking idea.

The ground can be kind of thin around here, John.

Thin?

Which means all you've to do is listen.

The van spins into the mist. Cornelius taps time on the wheel. John is not used to the company of males anymore. All the musk and hilarity and contest. Slate-grey to sea-green, the hills fall away. Melancholy, too, can gleam, jewel-like—as in the rain's sheen that blackens stone—and Cornelius steers blithely, and he beats time with his thumbs, and he turns happily—

Tell me just the one thing, John.

Yes?

Why's it you want to go to this little island?

Because I want to be that fucking lonely I'll want to fucking die.

Cornelius jaws on this for a bit and winces, and he nods it through—he is at length satisfied.

I have you now, he says.

The blue-bleak hills. The veiling of the fog.

This is just what I'm after, John says.

He is all business now—

About a boat and supplies?

Do I look like the fucken boy scouts, John?

The tape chews and a country song sticks hard on a high note and yodels; Cornelius pops the tape free and slaps in another; he throws a dark look seaward.

I'd doubt we'll be putting out in that.

Bit choppy?

He whistles through his nose; he sucks his teeth.

We'll keep you hid till the pressmen clear, John. We'll wait out the assault.

I haven't got all bloody year!

They'll want for patience. If they don't get the smell of you in a day or two, they'll be gone.

Just hole me up at a different hotel then.

Hotels no good. Too easy follow you out from a hotel. How'd you think they got wind of you in the first place?

You don't mean our woman in Newport?

Well.

Fucking Hatchet-Face!

The same woman has two husbands buried in the one plot, John. A small bit of respect would be no harm.

He massages the bridge of his nose—the painful place.

So where do I go, Cornelius?

I'm thinking the best thing for now would be my own house.

Super.

The van climbs and on a sudden turn, at a height above them, a silver horse in full mantle—its eyes shaded—is formed from the motes of air and mist and rises on its hind legs and makes a great silent scream—something Hispanic here—and its teeth are yellowish, foam-flecked, pointed, and it evaporates again, just so and as quickly, this image or vision, into time and the sodden air.

Cornelius?

Yes, John?

———

They climb into the sky. There are woeful songs about lost sweethearts, lonesome moonlight, dead fucking dogs.

It's coming between us, Cornelius.

The which?

The fucking music.

Cornelius slaps eject and the cassette pops—he flings it to the dash.

Thank you very fucking much.

You're very fucken welcome.

They climb some more—the country falls away.

As a matter of fact the van knows the road, Cornelius says.

A street gang of sheep appear—like teddy boys bedraggled in rain, dequiffed in mist—and Cornelius bamps the hooter—like teddy boys on a forlorn Saturday in the north of England, 1957—and the sheep explode in all directions and John can see the fat pinks of their tongues.

Mutton army, he says.

They climb the hills inside a cloud. Crags poke through; knuckles show. They come on a patch of clear blue for a stretch and he can see for the first time Clew Bay entirely and the way its tiny islands are flung out by the dozens and the hundreds.

It's been nine fucking years . . . How the hell are we going to find my island, Cornelius?

With enormous difficulty, John.

His stomach loops against the bumps of the road. His stones ache and tighten. He rolls the window for some air.

The bloody damp, he says.

And his bones remember Sefton Park as a kid—

Wet jumper.

Chest infection.

Irish Sea.

The van climbs. They are inside a cloud again. They are up and about the knuckles of the hills—it's the bleakest place on earth.

All this is O'Grady land, Cornelius says. Not that you'd feed the fucken duck off it.

An old farmhouse rises up from the hill—ramshackle, ill-kept, a growth on the hill. The van eases to a stop and a slow, deep-breathing silence. The house sits in complete agreement with its sad hill.

Fucken place, Cornelius says.

The wind drops and there is dead quiet—

Nothing moves.

Not a bird does sing.

The house was my father's before me. And you know he never so much as shaved in the house?

Oh?

Nor shat, John. He would have thought it dirty.

Emotion is about Cornelius like a black cloak now—

Oh my poor departed father . . .

His voice almost gives.

Death be good to him, he says.

He sighs and consults his belly and whispers a fast prayer.

They threw away the fucken manual, he says, after they designed my father.

Silence; a slow beat.

He turns to look at John carefully for a moment—

Could you handle a shave yourself, maybe?

I think maybe I could.

I see you go reddish in the beard?

When it comes through, yeah. I'm a gingerbeard.

I'm sorry for your troubles, John.

————

They sit together by the fireplace. The wind is high and plays oddly in the chimney. His heart stirs and searches for home again. On a sour, lonesome note the air moves through the hollows of the chimney and the house; the old house sighs and breathes. He sits inside this heaving thing, this working lung—how the fuck has he got here, and why? Cornelius slowly turns one thumb about the other and looks at him.

Would you be a saddish kind of man, John?

He answers in all the truth he can muster—

As a matter of fact, I don't think I've ever been happier.

Then what's wrong with you?

I suppose I'm afraid.

Afraid of what?

That all this happiness is going to rot my fucking brain.

Cornelius grins, stretches, rises.

Would you eat, maybe?

You know I think maybe I would.

Right so.

Cornelius goes to his cupboards and roots out a wheel of black pudding the size of a fat toddler's arm.

Cornelius?

But he moves with such dainty grace about the kitchen it's hard to speak against him. Like a small bear on casters he moves. He puts a pan on the stove. He cuts a chunk of lard in. The hot Zs of the sizzle come up to fill the room. He slices up the black pudding and sets the slices on the teeming fat. Watching this routine makes John feel calmer somehow. There is blood and smoke on the air. Cornelius fills the kettle and sets it to boil. He is strangely mothering in his movements. As in men who live alone. He arranges everything neatly and flips the slices of pudding over and John's mouth cannot but water.

You know I don't eat this stuff?

Never?

Not for fucking years.

He smiles and sets a place with care and plates the food and serves it with slices of bread cut thickly from the pan and a soft butter spread over.

Now for you, he says.

Jesus Christ, John says.

He eats the food. The spiciness, the mealiness, the animal waft—it's all there in the history of his mouth, and he is near to fucking tears again. The tea is strong and sweet and tastes of Liverpool.

Would you believe, John, that my father lived in this house till he was eighty-seven years of age?

How'd you get to be eighty-seven up a wet hill in Mayo?

He neither drank nor smoked.

I'm packing away all that myself.

I drink, John. I smoke. And I tup women.

Oh?

When I get the chance.

Cornelius slowly teases out the knuckles of one hand and then the other.

But you see what my father had was great intelligence.

That would help.

Oh he was a wiley man, John.

He was fucking what?

He was wiley.

What the fuck is wiley?

He was full of wiles, John.

He was full of fucking what?

He had a wiliness.

Oh . . . Like in he was canny?

Exactly so.

Okay. So now I have it. But tell me this, won't you—how can you have a windy fucking moor that's wiley?

Hah?

How can you have a wiley fucking moor?

A wiley . . .

He sings it for him in a witchy screech—

Out on the . . . wiiiley . . . windy moors . . .

What's it you're saying to me, John?

The Kate bloody Bush song!

Kate Bush?

Cornelius shakes his head.

I knew a Martin Bush, he says.

Oh?

Belmullet direction but long dead and God rest him, poor Martin.

Any relation?

To who?

To Kate bloody Bush!

I didn't know a Kate. Could she have been a sister?

She might well have been.

No . . . I knew a Martin.

And was he wiley?

If there was one thing he wasn't was wiley, John.

Oh?

Poor Martin was an inordinately stupid man. He could barely tie his shoelaces.

A ha'penny short?

Ah listen. Martin kept animals had more wile in them.

What kind of animals?

He'd sheep. A few cattle, I suppose. Though they'd have been wind-bothered up that way.

They'd have been . . .

Bothered, John. By wind coming in. The way it would unseat cattle.

Unseat them?

Cornelius lowers his sad eyes—

In the mind.

You mean you'd have a cow'd take a turn?

Cornelius squares his jaw.

Do you realise you're looking at a man who's seen a cow step in front of a moving vehicle? Purposefully.

On account of?

Wind coming easterly. That's the kind of thing that can leave a beast beyond despair. Because of the pure evil sound of it, John. The way it would play across the country in an ominous way. An easterly? If it was to come across you for a fortnight and it might? Sleep gone out the window and a horrible black feeling racing through your fucken blood. Day and night. All sorts of thoughts of death and hopelessness. This is what you'd get on the tail end of an easterly wind. Man nor animal wouldn't be right after it.

John pushes back his plate and sups the last of his tea and idly twirls the rind of the black pudding about the dull silver of the tines of his fork.

Cornelius?

Yes, John?

Am I alive and not dreaming?

He taps once and sharply the fork on the edge of the table for tune—it rings cleanly.

———

He walks a circuit of the O'Grady yard. He is high anxious again. His fucking jailyard. He circles and twists like an aggravated goose. Energy is the difficulty always. Too much of. An excess of. Flick out these fingers and they might shoot beads of fire. One neurotic foot in front of the other, and circling—what you do is you keep moving. He limps and he stumbles—no stack-heeled Harlem glide is this—and his bones ache; the sky above is grey and the wind moves the clouds over the bleak hills and the fall-away fields. The stone walls drunkenly wander the hills on unmentionable escapades. All is pierced with anxiety and dread. It's the place of the old blood and it has too a sexy air.

The sexy airs of summer.

From who and where was that? At difficult angles across the hills the grey sheep move. They drift unpredictably like the turns of his own dark, glamorous mind. The past is about, too, but now it's the more recent past, and he imagines the salve again of (oh-let's-say) heroin, and how might that feel, John? To fall into that dream again—to be in the arms of the soft machine again—and to have that deeper quiet and space again. Morpheus, the dream. Noise is the fucking difficulty always. The excess of. The wind licks out the corners of the yard—its tongues move in green darts and lizard-quick. Sexy airs. Wasn't it from Auden? The wind speaks, too, and in urgent whispers. News from far-out? Or from close-in? He shakes his head as he walks and circles the yard, and he notes from the corner of his eye the presence of Cornelius by the farmhouse door, leaning against the jamb, and his eyes are vast with pleasantness. The arms folded. The bull's head inclined. The expression of great interest.

John?

Yes, Cornelius?

You know what I'd wonder sometimes?

What's that?

If I amn't half a blackman.

———

Cornelius carries with prim importance two shaving bowls and two razors. They climb to a tin-sided outhouse built into the rocks of the hill. The outhouse lacks a door and John can see down the country as the sky moves its clouds along and the sun appears and it's trippy now in the sunburst. The fields are lit and lifting. It's the hour for a shave and a philosophic interlude.

A black, Cornelius?

Is fucken right.

I think I see where you're coming from.

Cornelius turns his throat and jerks the head curtly.

I'm talking if we were to go way back, he says. I'm talking from the south.

Cornelius rinses off the razor and shakes it dry. He slaps his face to get the blood back in. The blood comes hotly in a rush to enliven the stately face. He leans against the rock and looks out on the freshening day as if it might just about contain him.

I'm talking about cunts off boats, he says. I'm talking about my father's father's father's father's father's time.

I'm losing track.

I don't know if we aren't looking at the likes of 1400?

As if it was the other Wednesday.

You're saying there might have been a dusky sailor back then?

Now you have me.

Do you hear whispers from back there, Cornelius?

Ah I would do. Yes.

You mean from an old life?

Back arse of time, he says, and gestures grandly with a sweep of imperious paw.

What do you hear?

I think it could be a class of Portuguese.

There's an old tar with a monkey on his shoulder. And what do you see?

This is where it gets good. I see a tiny window set deep in a thick stone wall.

Yes?

With four iron bars set hard in the sill.

You were in a spot of bother then?

I would think so, John, yes.

Involving?

Nothing fucken good. Horses, definitely. And somehow I think a plain girl but gamey and with greenish eyes.

He calmly shaves. The burn of his jaw is a cool ordinary feeling and the afternoon is calm and bright or at least it is for a while. Cornelius considers him carefully and for a slow, held moment—

You have the longish nose, he says. Like a particular type of dog I can't place.

———

Sometimes in the black oily panic of the night when the city sent unsettling dreams across its towers and violent bowers—

the shapes of night in the park
the dark trees crouching
the trees so fiercely bunched
these creatures about to spring

—it was then he would travel to the island in his mind, and he would quieten when he lay his sore bones down among the rocks for a while and let the water move all around and the sky hang down its cold stars—its cold, cold jewels—its stars.

Cornelius?

Yes, John?

I want to get to my fucking island.

I know that, John.

I want a boat and a tent and fucking supplies and I want to be brought to my fucking island and then I want you to fuck off again for three fucking days. I mean that's all I fucking ask! Is three fucking days a-fucking-lone!

If we were to move now we'd have a pantomime on our hands. The pressmen?

Paranoia oozes in black beads from the tips of his fingers—the day has carved his nerves up bad.

He is fearful and dizzy and cutting off from the real again. The Maytime comes at him like razor blades.

You're eating the fags, John.

Evening sidles up to the window to taunt the parlour room. He smokes and he drinks a mug of strong tea.

Would you look crooked at an egg, John?

You know I nearly would.

He eats a boiled egg with soldiers of toast and at once he's brave as a trooper. It's a duck egg of maiden blue. He sings a bit and it's got a yodelled twist on the line, a duck's waddle in the quaver.

Lovely, Cornelius says.

He spoons up his egg—maiden?—and sups his tea. He feels like he's moved into a nursing home. And not before time.

Cornelius paces the stones of the floor, gravely, but now he stops up short.

Time have we, John?

I don't know the time.

We'll chance it.

They sit in front of the television—a tiny black-and-white with a clothes hanger stuck in—and they are just in time—Cornelius

twists the set precisely to align it with the stars—because the
music strikes up, and Cornelius nods in satisfaction.

Muppets, he says.

———

You know they've wanted me on?

Who, John?

The Muppets.

Ah yeah.

They've made approaches three fucking times.

Cornelius grins.

Okay, he says.

Honestly.

I see.

For real!

Cornelius thinks about it for a bit, and shrugs.

I suppose they had Elton John on the other week.

No surprise there.

He was superb, John.

Did you really, really think so?

I did.

No accounting.

Are you going on, John?

I'm not.

Why not?

It'd be too fucking whimsical. Anyway the technical fact is I'm retired, Cornelius.

Hah?

And not being a dry arse but it'd be too light. You've got to play along with all the routines. You've got to do the hokey cokey with Miss fucking Piggy. You've got to do all the wise-cracks with the frog. And to be honest, Cornelius, I don't know if I'm in the mood these days.

I think you should go on, John.

Really?

What harm in it?

Well . . .

It might take you out of yourself, John.

I suppose it might.

———

Night drags itself across the hills like a weary neighbour, acheful and slowly, one drugged foot at a time, and he takes— himself wilting—to the dead father's room. It is a room hushed with odd feeling and the boards creak beneath his monkey feet. As he settles between the ice-cold sheets, there are streaks of grey light still in webs across the Maytime. He drags a curtain against the world and sky. The ocean is out there, too, and moving—he can hear it as he puts his head down, and he wishes again for love and home. He falls at once to a heavy, troubled sleep.

Why should I run the way that I run?

———

He wakes to an unknown darkness. He is unsettled by a dream. Its shapes hold for a moment but fade as quick. He comes up to himself slowly, as though through dark water. He is in the dead father's room. Okay. There is a wardrobe full of old suits. It sits there like an accusation. All burly-shouldered and dour, this wardrobe. Now this was a life here once, as though to say. The arms and the legs of it. He feels that meek in its presence. He sits up in the bed. The wind rises and moves through the house again. He gets up from the bed and parts the curtain and looks on down the night. It is so clear and all the stars are out. He looks on down the sky, the way it falls away from the mountain, the night-blue and gasses, which is tremendous to a man in his T-shirt and shorts at four in the morning. Oh but that fucking wardrobe. The wardrobe is a presence in the room.

Don't be scared, John.

He goes to the wardrobe. He runs his hand through the suits in there. It gives a shivery feeling. He takes one out. It is very old and heavy. A word appears in his mouth—worsted. An old-fashioned word—two slow farmer syllables. *Wor-sted.* West Country farmer. Pebbles in the mouth. *Wooor-sted.* The material is a silvery blue in the night. The suit looks as if it would be a fit or just about.

Death be good to him, he says, and he slips an arm into a sleeve. He shucks the other in—it's perfect. He tries the trousers and they go on just right, too. He tries out the voice in a whisper then—

Well?

He is up the hills. He has a black collie with a patch eye. He has a great knobbly blackthorn stick. The dog runs the edges of the field that fall down to the stone walls and sea.

He whistles for the dog. He can hear him come back through the long wet grass. He can hear his panting and the parting of the grass. The bay beneath is so placid. He pulls back the wardrobe door for the mirror inside, for the dark-stained silver, and he stands before it, and cries—

Darkie! C'mere, Darkie!

Cornelius appears in the doorway and is pale himself as the risen dead.

John?

Yes, Cornelius?

How did you know the dog's name?

———

Look. There is nothing for it, John. It's half past midnight and the clock doesn't lie. Sleep is shot and sleep is done for. You have the whole house woke. We'll have to go out for a while. There is nothing else for it. We'll go and have a few drinks and try relax ourselves.

At half past twelve?

They'll only be getting going above in the Highwood, John.

Above in the fucking where?

Part Two

LADY NARCOSIS
(SWEET COUNTRY MUSIC)

There is a show tonight in the Highwood, John. There will be all sorts of people to play music there. We must go tonight to the Highwood, John. We'll breathe in the music and the cold-starred air.

———

And Cornelius has taken down the moon—hasn't he?—with gleam-of-eye and giddying snout and his touch on the wheel is delicate as the spring, here a soft tip, there a glanced tap for each swerve of the road as it runs the country and turns.

Oh this is the knack of it—John can see clearly now—the carefree life, and he envies him the spring.

And before we know it, John? The summer proper will be in on top of us and the woods will be whispering.

Fuck the whispering woods, Cornelius. Just get me to my fucking island.

But he is snagged again; he turns helplessly.

How'd you mean, about woods?

Cornelius beams—

There are things we can't describe, he says.

Go on?

What we see around us is only at the ten per cent level, John.

Of?

The reality.

And what's the leftover?

Unseen.

How'd you mean?

Well, he says. The way sometimes you'd walk across a field and a sense of elation would come over you. Are you with me?

Okay . . .

You're half risen from the skin. The feet are not touching the stones. The little heart is about to hop out of your chest from sheer fucken joy. And the strange thing about it?

Go on.

That patch of happiness could be floating around the field for the last ten years. Or for the last three hundred and fifty years. Out of love that was had there or a child that was playing or an old friend that was found again after a long time lost. Whatever it was, it caused a great happy feeling and it was left there in the field. You're after walking into it. And for half a minute you're lifted and soaring but then you're out the far side again and back into your own poor stride and woes.

You'd find a sadness just the same?

Or an evil, John. Or a blackness. Or terror, John, or fucken terror, because there's plenty of terror in the world. Always was and has been.

A soft whisper—

I mean take a look out the window.

A sweep of the arm for the greys and sea-greens of the moon-full hills, the pale night as they pass by—

I mean why'd you think I've the fucken foot down, John?

———

In the darkness of a sudden valley the van is brought to a halt. Its engine ceases apologetically. Cornelius raises deli-cate business—

The suit is fine. I'll say again I'm inclined against the running shoes. But here . . .

He presents a tub of hair cream:

A pawful of this gentleman, John.

He greases back his hair. He checks his look in the rearview. He arranges a fag in the corner of the gob for a spiv's face, a nylon-dealer's—he has a Second War face.

Take the spectacles off, John. Thank you. Now try these boys for me?

Bloody hell.

My poor dead father's prescription-issue. The misfortunate man couldn't see his own hand half the time nor the plate in front of him.

The lenses are so thick the world comes down to just blurs and vague shapes. Everything is abstracted. He climbs out of the van. He is close to moving water. It is a warm night in the Maytime. The dark water laps. He looks over the tops of the glasses and examines his reflection in the van's window. Cornelius climbs down for an inspection also and at once chokes back a sob.

John?

Yes, Cornelius?

You're the fucken bulb off him.

———

Your name is Kenneth.

Kenneth?

You're home from England. You're the first cousin on my father's side. You don't talk much.

Oh?

On account of a brutal speech impediment.

And what does K-K-Kenneth do in England?

He works in a car factory in Coventry and is married to Monica and does the pools of a Saturday.

———

Look. We are all terrified, John. There is no mystery to it. If you weren't terrified, there would be something wrong with you. The world is a hugely uncertain fucken place. Things can go either way and at any time. Step out of the bed in the morning and there is no guarantee you will step back into it the same night. The whole of your life is up in the wind and it might take off in any direction. We are all terrified at least half the fucken time. So what matters? For a finish? If we are all terrified and if it all ends in hell and misery and roaring fucken death anyhow? I'll tell you what matters. How you hold yourself is what fucken matters. How you walk through the world is what fucken matters. The set that you have of the shoulders. That's what matters. Is the chin held up in the air and proud or is it sunk down on the chest like a frightened little pup? That fucken matters, John. It's all a gamble. We have no control. We have no hope. We haven't a prayer against any of it. So throw back the shoulders. Comb the hair. Polish the shoes. Never let a plain girl pass by without compliment. Keep the eyes straight and sober-looking in the sockets of your head. Look out at the world hard and face the fucker down. And listen at all times, John. Do listen to what's around you.

———

Cornelius?

Yes, John?

When was it you adopted me?

The shyness of the smile; the fondness in the eyes—

I'm not sure when it was exactly.

———

The van is parked by the roadside. John is all angles in the phonebox. He is getting an earful. Cornelius passes into the phonebox the 5p pieces and the 10p pieces—John feeds them to the phone like prayer tokens.

Across the ocean the signals travel and their voices.

At length Cornelius shakes his head and makes the sign of a slit across the throat.

Because sometimes, John, a man has to attend to matters he has been called to.

The ground beneath them feels hollowed out and deep.

———

And the season is at its cusp, as if this is the night precisely that spring will give way to summer, as if it is all arranged in advance, at celestial council, and the world soon will throw back its doors and open out its moments.

It becomes for him a sedative night. The world moves slowly on its chains. Car lamps range their lights all over the mountain—the lights are thrown slowly and move. A breath of wind moves the trees as softly and the hedges. There are people aiming for the Highwood from just about everywhere. They tunnel into the dark by their lamps.

The sky above is starless and discreet behind clouds, and along the flank of the mountain the van moves quickly and climbs. Cornelius slaps down a cassette for mood—a heart-

broke voice picks sentiment from the air and yodels it dread-
fully.

Cornelius?

Ray Lynam, John. That's what I'd call a fucken singer. The
way he holds the note and wouldn't be caught looking for it?
Superb.

———

They leave the heavy airs of the sea behind. They are headed
for the Highwood. It is lost somewhere in the hills.

The worst thing you can have, John, is an empty night in
front of you. You're as well to fill up the nights always.

He unscrews the lid from a bottle of Powers whiskey and
passes it.

Tip the glanced wheel, the road is turned; John takes a beady
sip.

Now, Cornelius says; the wheel is tapped.

And the lamps bring up the graven rocks and the gaps in the
hills and the great ferns that blur in the light wind, and the
wind this high holds a thousand voices, trapped.

What's the feeling you'd get hereabouts?

Better not to ask, John.

Bleakish?

It would incline you to open your wrists in a running bath.

Oh?

There was never anyone who was right around this stretch.

It's not just me then.

The van moves quickly and climbs.

There's one of us as badly off as the next always, John. That's the great happy thing to remember in life.

Empathy—oh send me just the one song.

————

They come at last to the Highwood. It is by the edges of a lake. It is set on a plateau. It is patrolled by skinhead crows grey-booted and stern. It is encircled by great pines. It is attended by ghosts but they are his own and not sombre. There are a few habitations strung out and about like misplaced teeth but they invite no questions. There is a long, low-sized pub that wears no signage. Strings of coloured lights spill gaudily from the pub. Cars in grievous repair are not so much parked as abandoned around the edges of the pub. The van is set down to keep company with them. There is a squall of dreadful music from inside the pub.

At quarter past one?

It'll be filling up soon enough, John.

The music from the pub is made of jangled strings, mania and a flute.

A throng of drinkers spills also from the pub. They have the look of difficult people. They are all elbows and accusation. Cornelius with satisfaction kills the engine and sighs.

Keep yourself to yourself, John, and you'll find this is a very discreet house.

The drinkers appear to be related or at least of a tribe. There is commonly a ranginess and a long-limbed look. There are eyes dark, deep-set and impenetrable. Feet have the tendency to be planted quite widely, as of gunslingers, or sheep shearers.

These are decent people, John. These are lovely, warm-hearted, respectable people. They'd have no more interest than the wall in poor apes out of bands.

They pass through the lake's air and time. They approach the evil pub. They dip for a low entry. They enter a groan of voices in the dim—

———

I see you have a nice little throat on you, Kenneth? When you get going at all?

He drinks some whiskey and laughs and he drinks some more. He takes a pint of stout in his hand. He has a nip of brandy. The world is just blurs and vague shapes. Mouths talk at him. Eyes come close. Night colours fill the hoods of eyes. He talks to a young man who looks like an old man and says he's a doctor.

Doctor Carl O'Connor, he says, rather grandly, and presents a firm, clean shake.

Our problem here, he whispers, and I speak from harsh experience, Kenneth, is the lip. I mean take the continental. The continental will enjoy a glass of wine with his supper and some pleasant conversation and then very happily go home for the evening. But the Irishman is familiar always with the concept of the lip. Are you with me?

I think I am.

The Irishman will have a glass of wine with his supper and it will be lovely but then he will say, oh fuck me now anyhow! Oh Jesus Christ almighty! I have the fucken lip on me now! And that'll be it for the night, Kenneth. He is gone.

You mean there's no "off" button?

Precisely so.

The night fractures and folds in.

——————

There is a hefty chap with a voice that sounds like gravel in a bean can, and he has only the one ear.

What's happened your other?

A badger got it, Ken.

Oh?

I was put out of my own mother's house on account of drink and the false accusation that I had masturbated into the fireplace after she had gone to bed one night. I had nowhere left to live. This went on for five months. May to September.

Like a romance.

It was no romance, Ken. I was sleeping in sheds. I was sleeping in the car park of the Regional Hospital. I got rickets and a bleeding ulcer out of it. I could keep down nothing stronger than milk.

You're not doing so bad now.

Well. Wait till I tell you. It was the way the ear went on me that turned my entire life around like a miraculous transformation. You might think there was drink involved but there was no drink involved. What was involved was buck fucken madness. On the night of the badger.

They move in shadows, don't they?

Well this is it, Ken. But if I hadn't come through that dark night in that field I wouldn't be stood here talking to you now.

———

Bodies move; the night shifts.

Someone sings a bit from the Beach Boys for half a minute—

Well it's been building up inside of me
for oh, I don't know how long.

Which is all he fucking needs, and for a moment the pressure of his sadness is vast on the note that holds.

Are you not so great in yourself, Kenny?

No, I'm not so great.

I thought as much.

He sits tightly in a corner and keeps his eyes down. The measure of the note that holds is brokenheartedness. Bodies sway; teeth sing. Smiles twist on gappy mouths. Heavy scowl lines show by the grimace and the grin. He watches a mandolin player collapse into himself and get carried out sideways.

Argument goes through the musicians like fire.

The burly landlord says—

Right. Be done with ye. A pack o' cunts.

And he turns on the radio instead.

Kate Bush is away on her wiley fucking moors still.

He calls to the landlord—

What's the station?

Luxy.

They like their K-K-Kate Bush.

Cornelius passes by and bites a woman's neck as he passes and she squeals and slaps.

Now, Cornelius says. Aren't you delighted?

The night fractures; it folds in.

There is wild talk that the singer Ray Lynam might show—he is known to be in the vicinity.

———

An older lady sits and clings to him for a while, auntishly. She carries a waft of marmalade and brandy. She tells him that she is out with the sister—her bird-like fingers claw at his forearm—that she hasn't talked to the sister in nine years, a nine years that is now lost to them—her nails dig into his skin—and there is no sign of a thaw—none whatsoever—and what it all goes back to is that she came down pregnant, the sister, and I said a stupid thing. Sometimes, Ken, a stupid thing can be a true thing but even so you shouldn't say it. I said is the child his? Referring to Ronnie. Well. Six months later didn't the yellow-faced child step out from her. And there was no prizes for guessing where that came from. Out of him from the fish farm. Out of him out of Belfast. Out of him in the denim the yellow child was spawned. Out of him with the big ignorant mouth on him and the same buck not knee-high to a fucken midget. And of course Missy hasn't spoke to me since. But what harm? Is there call, when you think about it, Kenny, for us all to be mouthing away at each other like fucken goats, morning, noon and night? Would it not be better for us all to shut up for a while and ease off on ourselves? Hah?

———

He stands by the doorway and smokes and looks out to the tall pines that shimmy and flex in the wind and to the dark lake's water as it laps. A pale youth stands beside him, a brightly eager type with his head inclined gently for questions.

This place around here is called the Highwood then?

No, Ken.

Oh?

The pub is called the Highwood.

So the place is named after the pub?

You could look at it that way.

————

Cornelius swings a great dog-faced laugh as he passes by. He seems to bark as he moves. The radio goes off again and everybody roars for a while and Cornelius is on the verge of tears he is so happy to see everybody.

Silence is requested and a shimmer goes through the room—is it Ray Lynam that's in? But no, there is no country singer, it is just a young girl that sings out to the tips of her black hair, and the night folds in around him.

Too much.

He goes outside for a while. It is starless now and black and the sky is breathing. The tips of her song vibrate and strain to fill the room back there—he closes his eyes to hear it.

Well it's been building up inside of me
for oh, I don't know how long.

The past opens to him as starlessly and dark. He walks from it and towards the water. He goes for a while into the feeling of being lovelorn and younger. That green envy, that deathly swoon inside, and say it's the year that you're seventeen.

If he can hold the feeling, maybe he can work from it again and write again.

———

He talks to a very old man. He says that age can come and go in your life, can't it?

Well, the old man says. I'm eighty-seven years of age now but I looked worse when I was seventy-three.

That's exactly what I mean.

There are some people, the old man says, who are not only old at forty but they're bitter aul' cunts, too. Do you know what I mean?

I surely do.

But there's no worry in that because they'll all get the fucken cancer.

———

He drinks some more. He smokes what is passed to him. The young dark girl sings again and he sits tightly in the corner and he listens to her sing and he settles to the belief of himself as an unknown and safe here, in the Highwood, as this soft-voiced Ken, with his old-fashioned hair and his milk-bottle eyes, and a suit that sweats and itches and smells of dogs, rain and coalsmoke.

He drinks a white spirit that is passed to him—by the fiery bead it goes down—and Cornelius swings by, madly grinning and able—

Cornelius in a burly fast Cornelius-type rush

—and he says hush! He says hush now, everybody, hush, for the love and honour of Jesus. Ah for Godsake hush! I think Kenneth might have a song for us?

And the remarkable thing is, Cornelius says, he don't stammer even the one time when he sings.

————

He is accused of stealing fags by a farmer.

The Gitanes!

They're me own fucking Gitanes!

You're only a stoaty cunt, the farmer says.

He is pinned to the wall—the farmer's great knuckly paw presses hard against a reedy art college chest.

You're only a long yella fucken stoaty cunt!

He shucks from the paw and screams—

Who's ever heard of a sheep farmer smoking fucking Gitanes?

The farmer falls to one knee like an old crooner and shows his palms in a gesture of injured righteousness just like Levi Stubbs out of the Four Tops and goes oddly falsetto—

I do smoke the fucken Gitanes! he cries on the high note.

And Levi Stubbs' tears run down his face.

———

Beyond the high window the sky moves its clouds and now clearly the night by the silver of its starlight shows—

The sceptred tops of the moving pine.

The shadow of a mountain as it reaches darkly for the sky.

———

He is called a stoaty cunt and a lying cross-eyed cunt and a Jew-nosed cunt and an English cunt, an English cunt, an English cunt.

The night folds in.

He drinks the white spirit and he smokes and he sings.

      ———

And now he is among the trees. He believes that he can talk to her across the night and trees. He tells her that he loves her. He says that he sees her sometimes in faces that pass by. He says that when he is near the sea he thinks of her most of all. He tells her what has become of him and I wonder can you see, he says, what might have become of us together. He says that he misses her still and badly and that he will miss her always. He says you were younger then than I am now. He says that he thinks of her as a girl still

my blue-veined love, my Julia.

      ———

Nausea sends him to his knees like a green-faced lout. He throws up in hot, angry retches. He lies on the bonnet of a car for a while and he looks to the sky above the hills. He feels the cool night around him as a second skin. He hears two men speak—the North-of-England is in their voices. He cannot see but can feel the way the men lean against the wall and smoke and talk and the way their voices gather thickly in the dark—

Kenneth? one says. Don't think so.

      ———

He sits in the corner of the pub and holds himself tightly. Time is not fixed down at all. He might be anywhere in life.

He might be down the art school. He might be down the boozer—Ye Cracke. Or in Hamburg where the brassers grin from the windows and wear army boots and black knickers and fire at him from toy machine guns as he goes past, turning the hoarse creaking rattles on the machine guns, rat-a-tat-tat. He smokes what is passed to him. The night stretches out its voices and yelps.

Keep it f-fucking down! he cries.

Kenneth, Cornelius says, would often take a sour turn late on in the evening. But there is no violent harm in him whatsoever.

A North-of-England voice is close by again; there is something darker here.

If you need a quiet place, John? Well there is a place called the Amethyst Hotel.

———

He walks through the trees for a while. He listens hard. There have been hangings from these trees. He can tell. He can hear the creaking rope and slowly now it swings. He listens to the voices that move through the trees. He can hear them clearly. There is a world unseen just beyond us here but he is not frightened at all. The voice of a girl moves through the trees by the Highwood and it is a long time ago but he can hear her still and her sex is a tiny, distant star—

my cold-lighted love.

———

The first of the morning comes across the trees. The lake hardens with new light. He wakes to a head throb—it hurts even to think. He cannot place himself, quite. It hurts especially to fucking think. He lies on his belly on the smooth stones by the edge of the lake. He feels great age down the reptile length of himself. He lies still and cold and listens to the water of the lake as it moves. He retches again. He has a pinhole in the centre of his forehead and all of the world's pain screams through. He is sweating fucking bullets. A flicker comes from the night at last. He turns painfully onto his back and sits—he sees the empty boarded pub, a grave jury of trees, the morning patrol of skinhead crows. Accusation in the yellow of their pin-bright eyes; he retches. Accusation in the black gloss of their coats; he retches. The night in flitters and rags comes back to him; he groans. Arrows of light are flung through the pines. He hears nearby a deep bovine suffering. He turns to find the van with its side door halfways open and a pair of boots stuck out at odd angles. He goes on his fours across the stones. He retches as he crawls and by slow evolution of the species at length brings himself to an upright stance and walks. He sets one monkey foot in front of the other until the van is reached. He pokes his head in back to find Cornelius red-eyed, purple-faced and lowing.

Cornelius raises the heavy solid head a martyr's inch and he looks with the most sorrowful eyes in the universe at his charge.

Fucken disaster, John, he says.

———

But of course another way of looking at it, says Cornelius O'Grady, is that things could not have turned out one jot better.

The O'Grady parlour room: Cornelius considers with happy eyes a mess of duck eggs.

The word'll spread quicker now that you're around the place again. That'll bring the whole game to a head, John. It might be the best thing could have happened us.

He reaches a hank of brown bread to the yolk of an egg. He chews, takes a swig of tea, chuckles.

Because what the fuckers don't know yet is that Cornelius O'Grady is running this game.

A sly grin; a wink.

Topping, he says.

John sits wretchedly by the fireplace; he shivers.

Cornelius?

Yes, John?

Did I really sing?

Cornelius widens his eyes to show fondness and awe; he whispers—

You were like a bird.

————

What fucking day is it?

The Friday.

I'm not even three days gone?

And doesn't it have the lovely hopeful air of a Friday?

Cornelius?

Things are looking good for the island, John.

He goes outside to the yard. He throws up again. It's the most extravagant gesture he's capable of. The day has come up wretchedly to a hot sun. The sun feels like jealousy on his skin. Cornelius comes and throws a pail of water to wash the sick away. Now there is a decorous or priestly air.

High up, on a clear day, and all of Clew Bay is presented. The knuckle of the holy mountain is far side. All of the islands are down there and waiting.

Cornelius sets beside him a mug of strong tea.

I've no willpower either, John. But I'm not going to give out to myself over it. God or whatever you want to call him puts these kinds of nights in our paths to test us sometimes. We failed the fucken test. But do you know the best of it? We'll be forgiven yet.

He is in busy whistling form as he marches about his business.

Cornelius? The last thing I'm in a condition to do right now is go sit on a fucking boat.

Drink the tea, John. You won't know yourself from Gandhi.

————

Though of course why you might want to go out to a mean little rock of an island is no one's business but your own. I'm only here to oblige you. We have always been an obliging breed of people, the O'Gradys.

Cornelius emerges from the house with a small, brown leather suitcase.

Supplies, he says. And if you don't mind me asking, John, what did you pay for the island? No mind. Your own business and no one else's. John is away to have a good long chat with himself outside on a wet fucken rock.

He shakes his head in wry humour and passes a bottle of Powers whiskey; it tastes like health.

The best of luck to you with it all. You're going to come away from Durnish in three days' time and do you know what?

A loving gaze—

You won't know yourself.

—————

The van drones and judders and turns now to show the glints of a grey sea. The sea is lazier than before. The knuckle of the mountain juts across the bay—

The holy mountain, he says.

Indeed, Cornelius says, and isn't generation upon end of decent Irish people after trotting up the cunt in their bare feet with their tongues hanging out of their heads and wind taking skin off them and rain coming hard and mud and shite and heart attacks and strokes being took by the new time and would you hear a single word of complaint from those dear pilgrims, John?

Eyes raised in soft questioning—

You would not, he says.

—————

The van stops on the coast road.

Ho-ho, Cornelius says.

Cornelius? Please. Let's just get to the fucking island.

Patience a small while.

Cornelius kills the engine. He climbs from the van. The wind comes harder now from the sea. He gestures for John to follow; he does. They walk the scalp of a hill together, descending.

You're not to be afraid, John.

They approach a great fall-away to the sea; far below, it flashes its green teeth, the ever-welcoming sea.

Right, Cornelius says.

He steps up to the edge; the fall is sheer—it's a great distance to fall and to a certain ending there.

Come on, John.

He steps with Cornelius to the edge of the sheer fall; the wind pulses hard against them.

Lean into it, Cornelius says. Like so.

He does and he is held there.

Fucking hell . . .

Be fierce, John.

The wind comes hard and Cornelius leans in closer again to its great force; he is held there.

Cornelius?

Now, John.

John tips his toes up close to the edge and closer again to the sheer fall and closer.

Cornelius?

Go on.

He leans over the edge and the wind holds him perfectly there.

Do you see, John?

Maybe.

Do you see the trick of it, John?

I think so.

No fear.

Part Three

EVERY DAY IS A HOLIDAY AT
THE AMETHYST HOTEL

The suitcase is ancient. It could be out of Lime Street station in 1925. Leather and belted; a stout little general. He wears the dead father's suit over his high-top purple trainers. The sun is psychedelic in hot streaks across the water. He looks back at himself from the water's surface. His eyes are glazed with shell-shock and paracetamol. The suitcase is by his feet and contains all of his supplies and somehow his aspirations. He worries a bit about this brown leather suitcase. Open it up and the past might tip out—

on rum parade.

I'm sorry, John?

Nothing, Cornelius. My mind is tipping out my mouth.

That would often be the way. Rum I never drank.

Cornelius rocks the boat free of its berth and aims it over the stones. He mutters blackly beneath his breath and swears vengeance against the waves and world. He pushes the boat out to the water. He works at the ropes and works at the motor—

Bastarin' fucken thing!

The seabirds hover watchfully with their mad eyes, all wing-span and homicide. He doesn't know the names for birds. Which is neither here nor there. He kneels down by the water to find his face come closer—

fuck me.

The shock of the age that's gone in. He looks older than Father fucking Time. Anxiety and fear and weight-of-love—these are the lines of his face.

Cornelius works the boat.

The motor catches and the rope unspools.

John climbs in and he almost falls but rights himself again—he's awkward as a duck.

The boat puts out to the water.

———

Tell me again, John.

Okay.

You're going out to this little island to scream?

I may well Scream.

You mean you're going to be roaring out of you?

It's certainly on the cards, Cornelius.

Like the crowd on Achill.

Oh?

But what's it all about, John?

Primal scream therapy was devised by Dr. Arthur Janov.

I never heard of him.

He lives in California. He has a clinic there. I spent three months with Dr. Janov. He taught me how to Scream.

What's it you'll be screaming about?

It's a technique for getting at buried pain and childhood trauma.

Why would you want to do that?

Because it weights you down.

And you want to be lighter on your feet?

Exactly so.

How light do you want to be?

How'd you mean?

What if you took off into the fucken sky?

You're stuck in your ways, Cornelius. You don't want to have your little world opened up.

My world's about as far a ways open as I can fucken handle. What kind of pain have you buried?

Same kind we all have.

On account of being a child?

Well . . .

We were all children, John.

I lost my father. He went away.

We all lost our fucken fathers.

I lost my mother. She went and died.

We all have the dead fucken mothers.

So tell me how you get by, Cornelius!

It's simple, John. I listen to what's around me.

Okay . . .

And then?

Yeah?

I react.

You listen. And you react.

Because everything you need in the world is there to be heard.

You have my interest, Cornelius.

You can see very little in this world, John. But you can hear fucken everything.

————

He lies down on the boards of the boat as it edges out and moves. He fixes the suitcase for a pillow. He falls back into the grey-blue sky and the day augments itself by patches of cloud and patches of blue as the boat moves out across the bay.

Abroad in the fucking world.

Beg your pardon, John?

He closes his eyes and listens hard—the world is full of hollows—and he is sixteen again and coming down Bold

Street—or maybe he's seventeen—and he wants to fuck everything that moves but he's in a fat phase and bevvied and he's headed for the last train at Central station and he bounces off every shop window—a staggering John—and he stumbles and falls into a doorway—Cripps department store—and the sky above the rooftops shows the woozy stars and he heaves and pukes and laughs like a dog as he wipes the sick away and weeps.

He opens his eyes.

The sky rolls out and moves.

He is left to his own private woes and the weaving of his miseries—he's an expert. Cornelius discreetly averts as John looks out and away, across the islands and the bay, and the boat dips and rises, and the engine judders, and the knuckle of the holy mountain jabs at the sky and the tiny islands are thrown about in all directions. He picks up a piece of dark wood like a baton and turns it—the way it feels snug and murderous in his hand.

The priest, Cornelius says.

For killing the fishies.

Or anything else might come at you.

Everywhere he looks there is another island but not his. All are familiar but none just right—

Well? says Cornelius.

No.

—because maybe the rocks are thrown about wrong or the way a hill runs at the sky is off. They pass another island and he sees a fast blur against the grey of the rocks and the movement is a quickness, a shiver, a silvering of the blood: the hare. They move farther out and the wind comes harder and in whippety slaps and he tunes into the slow boom and drift. The boat draws a curve around the tip of an island and comes on an open stretch of water. Across the colours of the bay they move and the way that his mood has lifted—now he's beaming and in tremendous good heart, it must have been the hare. He is coming close in.

This feels right.

But in the near distance another boat moves on the water, and draws closer, and there are dark figures in a blur, crouching.

I can see lenses.

Down, John.

He lies flat to the boards of the boat.

Fuckers. Stay down, John.

Cornelius works slowly to turn the boat—it drifts again.

Stay down.

He lies hardly breathing on the boards of the boat.

There's only one thing for it.

Yeah?

We'll have to go and see our friends on Achill.

———

Paranoia drifts in white smoke across the sky.

The boat moves.

And here's Cornelius—

his back to the May sun,

his face dark in shade,

his voice hoarse with soft cajole.

We should have headed here in the first place, John. There are no two ways about it. The Amethyst Hotel would be the very best place for you to wait out the assault.

The fucking where?

The Amethyst, John. On Achill.

Amethyst again? What the fuck is the Amethyst?

Sweet Joe's place.

Who the fuck is Sweet fucking Joe?

Now on Achill Island generally, John, you'll find the people are mean-spirited and small-minded and very aggressive. Tough nuggety foreheads on them. Hard lines to their faces. Tight little mouths. But of course this is no surprise in the wide earthly world . . .

He spits.

. . . because they've been jawing rocks at the side of the fucken road since the Lord Jesus was a bare-arsed child. We'll have nothing whatsoever to do with the Achill people, John. That's a promise to you and faithful. But the people where we're headed are not Achill by the blood. No indeed. They are your own kind.

The boards of the boat groan and sing.

The cliffs of Achill rise up ahead.

Paranoia races its squadron gulls.

Who exactly are these people, Cornelius?

The people, he says, who have taken over the Amethyst Hotel.

Something odd, something familiar—Amethyst?

———

Cornelius works the boat between the rocks. The motor cuts; the boat is tied off. He is helped from the boat by a great knuckly paw. Which makes him feel lady-like and fey and just shy the parasol. They come from the water and climb. They walk an old track hemmed in by singing hedges in the breeze. The feeling near and near-abouts is medieval. The growth everywhere is very fucking alive—it makes a sore pulsing in his throat. On Achill there is the throb of big summer coming and everything breathes. In the Maytime we are untethered and time is not fixed. Or so he believes. The world is in a high, sexy mood. Tiny fists of dread are bunched beneath his skin. He is on Achill Island again—a bad-trip place—and the light is harsh and he is cold with fear.

I've been here before, he says.

We've all been here before, John.

I'm not talking philosophic. I mean this fucking place. I've been here before.

They climb a bit and then some more. They come in quick time to the Amethyst Hotel. It's a strange hacienda in the Maytime sun. There are armies of insects on the island's air. And there are voices—listen?

The voices are high, wired, freaky.

I think I've been to the Amethyst fucking Hotel and all.

He steps through the pools of a lost dream now—it's been nine years since.

They pass through an old garden once formal but gone to seed and wild again and there is the feeling of things unseen travelling behind the hedges.

Sweet Joe, says Cornelius, is the gentleman that runs the Amethyst nowadays and I'd have to say he's an outstanding individual.

John is worried.

Sweet Joe, says Cornelius, would mind a mouse for you on Piccadilly Circus.

I thought we'd said no hotels?

Amethyst is not open to the public anymore, John. As such. It is for Joe and his friends' use only at this moment in time.

His friends?

The voices come up again. They are loud and desperate. He can hear unwellness and rage. He knows these voices at once and right off for what they are.

They'll know to expect us, John. We spoke last night. They know we might be stuck. These are your own style of people precisely.

It's true there are some old familiars on the air—

He can smell the fucking and the freebase.

He can smell the mania.

He can smell the freaks.

————

When he sees high the red letters raised

AMETHYST

on the white gable wall, it comes back to him for sure: he has definitely been here before. It's the nine years since. Some actors had it back then. They kept a very nice white wine. They had some quite good pot. They made us a picnic here. It was just a sweet nothing day. It was early in our life together.

The picnic was brought to the hills. The hills were scratchy with heather and nettles about the ankles and they sat for a while on a Scotch blanket and looked down on the slow-moving green-into-blue of the bay and ate tiny triangle sandwiches of cheese and pickle and drank the cold white wine—

didn't we?

—until the rain came in a sudden attack from a very irksome old god and they scurried away again as the sky changed colour quick as love can change and there was rain in their

faces and everything was giddy as hell and they were collaps-
ing with love.

There's another we'll never have back, he says to himself,
being the sentimental Scouse.

————

Inside. The air of the strange hotel is humid and trapped.
There are voices upstairs. They are going at it fucking hard.
There are footsteps now and a figure at the top of the stair—a
dark shade there.

Dips his head for a view—

Sweet Joe, Cornelius says.

The beast grins down the stair beneath a cloud or an aura
of bushy auburn hair. He has tiny yellowish pisshole-in-the-
snow-type eyes. But otherwise this is a most graceful fatman
on the move. The way that he bounces on the balls of his feet
as he turns the stair.

Fucking hell, John says.

The way that he has the look of an enormous forest hog—a
creature only rumoured, never seen. He wears a flowy
Victorian shirt that billows poetically and some kind of
breeches—*fucking breeches?*—and his skin has a high, health-
ful, vivacious glow. He is terribly fucking alive. He whispers
these decorous words—

How absolutely proper it feels to have you here, John.

His voice?

North-of-England.

————

Are you a little cold, John?

His voice—the North-of-England, the wheeze, the husk and Burnley of it.

I'm fine, thanks.

They sit in the hotel kitchen over a brew of nettle tea and fags.

We can get that chill in Maytime yet, the evenings.

There is something old-timey about his voice, as if transmitted from the days long since; there is a static on the coils of it. His face is alive with tics and nervy flutters as if there are small desperate birds trapped beneath the skin.

You'd need your cup of tea, he says.

Common-sensical, also, the tone, like a fucking busman, and there are arcane symbols daubed on the kitchen walls—

Black Sun,

Pentacle,

Evil Eye.

There are voices upstairs—young, unsettled, roaring.

Frank and Sue, he says. They're in the thick of it just now.

Oh yeah?

They've gone deepish, he says. We'd best not disturb Frank and Sue just now.

A rueful, confiding grin, and the words again are whispered—

They've been weeks getting to where they are now, Frank and Sue.

One minute they're roaring at each other, Cornelius says. The next they're riding each other like dogs.

It could go either way yet, Joe says, for Frank and Sue.

The voices above are pitched high and sorely and break at times to screeches, at other times to screams—John is back in a freakhouse again. It's been a stretch of time. He sips not unhappily at his nettle tea.

How's it you've ended up out here, Joe?

Oh it's hardly an ending, really, is it?

A flush creeps up the fatman's neck.

You can really listen out here, he says. I mean if it's a Mesmeric you're after.

Now, Cornelius says, and he tips a measure of Spanish brandy to each of their mugs, the three.

That'll keep the blood moving, Joe says.

Common-sensical, which is the true note of a madman, or so Peter Sellers said one time, and he'd have known.

Joe moves lightly on his feet to look out the window. He considers the Maytime in the island's gleeful light. He nods and turns.

It was magic last night, John, he says. You were there and you were not there.

Okay.

And you sang quite beautifully, actually.

I did?

But what a very strange song it was.

A song?

It was odd, Cornelius says, but it was lovely.

Okay, John says.

The night will not come back except in slivers and scraps and dark shapes that hover but will not hold.

On the walls—

the Hexagram,
the Ankh,
the Eye of Providence.

He is here and he is not here; he throws his palms down to slap his thighs, as though jauntily, but in fact for confirmation of flesh and bone, here on a hardback chair, in the kitchen of the strange hotel, in the month of May—how merry, how merry—in 1978.

How do you pass the days out here, Joe?

Exploration, he says. We dig in.

Oh yeah?

They'd be hammering each other, Cornelius says.

It has been there all the while but only now is he aware of Moroccan-type music on a hi-fi but faintly, a sitar, soft padded drums, and Joe smiles and shimmies his fat hips.

We go in hard at the Amethyst, John.

He sips his nettle tea and the brandy's warm kick comes through; he lights a fag for a prop. It's 1978, he's a bloody dad again, and he's away in a fucking freakhouse?

Where's it you're from, Joe? Originally?

Knowleston way.

Where?

But Joe just waddles a grin about his face and moves his fleshy hips to the desert music—languid, his fat rhythm. He looks at John calmly and evenly—

They call me Joe Director, he says.

He smiles, hog-like, and shows the graven palms—

Daft kids, he says.

There are no directors out here, he says.

We are very much a community out here, he says.

Oh yeah, John says, a community?

The Community of the Black Atlanteans.

Of the fucking what?

Upstairs, by now, the noises are unmistakably sex noises—

Hot shrieks.

Chocolate moans.

Livid whelps.

Frank and Sue, says Joe. They're young still and they have the blood for it, John.

Like dogs on the street, Cornelius says.

Is it just the three then?

There are other young friends who come and go, Joe says.

I bet there are.

But for now? Yes. A family of three.

He's been set down in a freakhouse; he eyes the blithe fiend Cornelius hard. But Cornelius just beams and aims splashes of brandy to each of their mugs, the three.

We go in deep out here, says Joe, and we go in all the way.

I have you, John says.

No stranger to the screaming himself, Cornelius says.

I understand so. But would this be along the lines of the California technique, John?

Well . . .

To scream is only the start of it, Joe says, 'round here.

His hog arrogance.

Oh yeah?

In fact we've gone a long ways past that 'round here.

Go on?

Around here, John, we get the rants on.

The rants?

Is fucking right. Have you ranted, John?

I can't say that I have . . . as such.

Joe Director purses his lips in regret; the bloody Lancashire of him.

The rants bring us all the way inside, John. And that's where we need to go, isn't it?

Best of luck with it, John says. I'm just on the way to me island.

Upstairs—the sound of a vaulting climax, and Joe lifts shyly an ear-cup for it.

Youth, he says, and smiles.

This is it, Cornelius says.

The vaulting cry lands; now there is a dull sobbing.

You set some people down on your island for a bit, John?

I did, yeah . . . years back.

I knew some of those people, John.

You did?

Oh yes, I did.

You by any chance know which island is mine, Joe?

I'd possibly know it by its air, John. I'm to understand from those people it has a very particular air.

Cornelius?

Yes, John?

When are we going to get to my fucking island exactly?

But Cornelius just smiles and shows a palm for patience and sips his brandied tea.

Joe Director gets the kettle on.

I'll brew up fresh, he says.

The sitars waft. A hurdy-gurdy, too. A clavichord? What's he mean, fucking particular? John wants to be a million miles from this place and he wants to be sat just where he is.

Outside—

low snaps of wind come from the sea to whip at the hedges and the pines.

In the Amethyst—

the dim jangle and spit of sitars,

the vaulted grunts and spasm breath of the fucking, renewed,

the brown burn of freebase, bitterly.

Tell me more about the rants, John says.

———

The life in New York runs along very tidy lines. He doesn't leave the apartment much. He doesn't need to—it's the size of fucking Birkenhead. He plays with the baby. He's that good the baby and sleeps like a turtle—he is that sweet in the shell. John looks out the windows. John barks at the cars. John eats sushi from cartons and watches the late movies in bed. Black-and-whites, he does all the movie voices—shut the fuck up, John! He gets eel juice on the sheets. He makes lots of plans. The days sail by and not ungaily. He sits on his backside. He sits in the great fortress high above the plain where the savage injuns roam. He's the Freaky Sheriff and he has a very beady eye. He bakes lots of fucking bread. The yeast and warmth of the kitchen on a cold winter day with the city under its heaps of dirty snow outside—he's cosy as a bastard in the womb. He is that happy he gurns and sings. And the days pass by and the nights and he cannot sleep if the wind is high and he looks out to the park and along the treetops the greens of the treetop fairies fly—hello? Words that come from out of the blue—arboreal. Which is lovely. He listens to the birds at dusk and all their newsy chatter. Like biddies at a bus stop. He gets nervous when the days get longer. He watches his weight. He doesn't drink booze and he doesn't do dope. He eats brown rice and baked fish and steamed veggies. He is decidedly on the leanish side—he turns side-on to the bedroom full-length for a profile check. He makes lots of plans. He smokes fags. He looks at the rain above the city and the lights caught and blurred inside the murk of the rain as the night comes down and it's an eerie docklight—he is home again. He develops certain arcane theories. He doesn't leave the apartment much. He makes certain occult connections. He gets worried about the number nine. He starts to have a thing about the elevator. He listens to strange music. He obsesses about the number fucking nine. He stays up all night. He reads about Stockhausen. He reads about Howard Hughes. He reads about what's-his-face, fucking Rimbaud. He watches bits of telly. He does all the telly voices. He is Greta Garbo. He is Captain America. He has mad energy sometimes and sometimes he has fucking zero. He is the Peanut Farmer Carter, he is Mao Tse-tung. Strange thoughts come unbidden—the world is full of hollows and the world is full of graves. Sometimes he plays the guitar but not often. He does all the telly voices—he is a cowboy, he is a spaceman, he is a pimp. He sends out for books on the occult. He talks on the phone to California, to Liverpool. He hums and coos and burps the baby—the baby spews. He sends tidy sums to radical causes. He is bone dry in terms of actual fucking songs is the sorry fucking truth of it all. He reads some Aleister Crowley—he's a right fucking laugh. He has zero fucking songs is the point of it all. He finds a channel that shows Monty Python at five in the morning. Baby spew the sour milk smell the bloody motherhood. He orders in. Bring us your raw fish and your pizza pie. One night he catches himself having a right good weep in front of a Pete-and-Dudley. He sits and looks across the sky and across the park and towers and it means nothing to him at all. He has no fucking songs. He is that happy he wants to Scream.

———

Violent confrontation, John.

This is Joe Director.

It's the only way to strip it all down and see what lies beneath. We've got to peel our skins back.

You reckon?

I do. And it's never easy. It causes a lot of pain. We've got to open up the clam shell. It's shut so very tight. I mean let's look at you, John. On the surface? Deviant genius.

Thank you very much.

But deep inside? I'd very much like to know. And I think you would, too, John.

From upstairs a dead velvety hush is loaded with the weight of their listening.

Sometimes it's difficult, John. I won't deny it. It can be very bloody difficult. We go in hard and we go to very tricky places. It can be deeply fucking unpleasant. But the rants can soften us, too, and sometimes we move very gently through the process. We can deal with tenderness. We can deal with love.

John fetches another splash of brandy for his mug of nettle tea. The bottle has an odd label in Spanish that shows a black lizard. Okay. The taste of fields in his mouth; the burn of the sexy brandy. Not unlovely.

The rants are unpredictable, John. Especially 'round here.

Joe Director: his grin soft with rue.

Cornelius: his face lit with happy wattage, an idea.

Mightn't it be the best place for you, John?

I beg your pardon?

I'll head for the mainland. I'll see who's around. I'll come back by the van and road bridge. I can see at least if the fuckers have cleared.

You're saying leave me here?

They wouldn't think to spot you at the Amethyst Hotel, John.

Outside the hills have collapsed into each other and the iron sea moves and he makes for another nip of the firewater.

Cornelius?

Yes, John?

When are we going to get to my fucking island?

Are you telling me you want to be sat there with eighteen thousand fucken cameras on you and the *News of the* fucken *World*? A few hours, John. I'll be back with the van and we'll be away.

Joe Director aims for a basement stair—

There's more where that brandy's come from.

He pauses, a bright notion—

Would you like to burn off some cocaine, John?

And from upstairs a sky-opening Scream.

Did I not tell you? They are your own kind precisely, John.

———

Frank and Sue?

He's a stunned-looking beanpole with matted blond hair in fag-ash ropes—a honky Rastafari. There is something canine or wolfish. As though born to the dog star. She's tiny and elf-eyed with busy, travelling tits. Attractive, a-gleam, but distant—an undiscovered star. North-of-England, the pair of them, but they are posher than Joe. There are pockets of coke burn on the air—bitter-grey and teasing—but the Amethyst Hotel more generally has the stale eggy waft of a fuckery. He sits down on the stairs with these kids and they have an earnest chinwag there.

You're on way to your island then?

That I am.

How big's it?

It's nineteen acres.

That's a spread is that.

Nineteen acres of rocks and bloody rabbit holes.

Not to mention the banshee fucking wind—he lights a fag. He has a sip of nettle tea. He has sworn off the lizard brandy and he has refused the base cocaine. He feels strong, wise, avuncular and glad.

This is it then?

How'd you mean?

Just the three of you here?

There are others that come and go.

I bet there are.

You sound a bit worried, John.

This was Frank.

Why should I be worried?

Sounds like you got the fear in.

Why should I have the fear?

I'm playing with you.

You're playing with *me*?

Sue darts a lizard tongue to lick at her tidy, full lips; Sue beams hard the elf lamps—

Why's it you've come here? she says.

I guess I'm running away, too.

From what? Frank says.

From who? Sue says.

From myself, he says. I'm gonna be the first in human history that manages to outrun his own fucking shadow.

They look at each other—he's dark, she's distant; their grins are way the fuck off.

What's it you pair are running from?

I was always going to come here, she says.

And me, Frank says.

It draws you in, she says.

It's got an air, he says.

Little runaways, John says.

You sound different, she says.

Different how?

Different older.

Well I'm thirty bloody seven, aren't I?

Posh kids gone west for dope and fucking and screeching—he knows their kind long since.

How's it you've found this Joe?

Their eyes go down at mention of Director.

You go at it hard around here, don't you?

She looks at the boy—he smiles, nods: they turn to kiss quickly and hard. And now she turns back to John and it is regretful, her smile, as though to say you will never know this taste.

Sue flicks the elf lamps; then—

We get the rants on, John.

———

There is no true dark in the Maytime on Achill—it might be an isle of Norway. He moves about the small dead hotel. There is a haze of blue light in the evening windows still. Frank and Sue weep loudly in a room upstairs; Joe Director is in the kitchen tending with homicidal cheer to a goat curry. John has entered the swim of family life at the Amethyst Hotel. That sweet clamminess. Cornelius has returned to the mainland to fight back the press dogs. There are statements daubed on the walls at the Amethyst Hotel—statements about the id, statements about tide of Capricorn. The carpets squelch underfoot and give off the stale aniseed waft of seawater. He is so many fucking miles from love and home. There are fiendish midges on the air and they swarm to attack his blood. Get it at the neck, get it at the font. He slaps the tiny Nazi fuckers away. Evidence of life, at least. He smokes, sighs. He stands in the doorway porch of the Amethyst Hotel, slapping lazily at the bugs, and he looks out to the half-lit night. Joe Director comes along to link arms, companionably. Joe Director has odd charisma. There is a blush of heat rising beneath the collar of his antique shirt.

Did you know that Mars is about, John?

Well that's all I fucking need, isn't it?

It is a dull fire in the eastern sky and now the past in a dark sliver returns: it was here they saw the women dressed in black walk into the sea.

_____

Scared but even so he goes for a turn in the half-a-night's air. Now it is Sue that comes to follow and watch. She is tiny as a faerie that could walk the leaves and not bend a stem but weirdly big up top with those giddy tits and she wears a Victorian brocade number for a blouse and she has her sexy smile on—hasn't she?—and she sits in the garden and tunes into the far-out stations.

Alright, Sue, love?

A smile, an elf's—she picks at the flowers. The half-a-night smells of salt and flowers. He watches the sheep for a bit. They drift this way and that across the crooked track that comes up the hills to the Amethyst, and loose sand moves in strange drifts and sings—a grainsong—and he's emotional—just a bit—and he walks the haunted hotel garden—he wants to get away from the freaky elf-eyes, from the North-of-England girl Sue—and now he is entirely unseen—or so he believes—and he looks down and trips out for a while on the slow-moving waves—birdsong, breath-of-sea—and he watches the salty Dummkopf sheep as they come and go, the way they move like slow daft thoughts, and his go to his old dad again. A flitter in the head and he is back in that place again. The way that he sneaks up sometimes unawares, the way he just appears—

Alright, Freddie? Alright, kid?

And always it's as a kid, he sees him as a kid in the faraway twenties—Little Freddie, of the Bluecoat orphanage, a gimp, he comes hop-a-long—and he sits on a rusted iron bench by the briars and the beads of the berries of the haunted island garden—treesong, breeze in the leaves, his blues, a midnight yearn—but what he feels beneath the pads of his feet are the stones of the city of Liverpool—as was, Mariners Parade, Fazakerley Street, Hackins Hey—and he watches the city and the world take all its strange forms and shapes through his father's eyes, and how it must have been for him, and how great the miracle, the zillion-to-one shot that his eyes should fall and catch on a slender girl, his blue-veined love, his Julia.

Dead love stories are what make us.

———

Well.

He's all stirred up. Just fucking leave it, John, he says.

By night the old garden is sweet as incense and hollow as a church. There is a great heaviness here. Tang on the air of the summer-come-soon, and with it the years are coming back—windy beaches, freckled youth, the thin reddish-brown limbs of a north-western summer; the summer of his lost anonymous England; Tropic of Lancashire. He speaks now in his old true voice. Feeling lurches; feeling shrieks. He cannot think about his father easily. It causes too much commotion. He'll have a fag and a brandy instead—tamp all that stuff down. That way you can keep the past locked in. He goes inside again. Sue comes along to follow and watch.

Okay, Sue?

In the lobby he falls into an old armchair. Damp green the velvet, like mosses, as if the world is creeping up through its stones and into the Amethyst again. He feels like a very senior citizen. Sue eyes him darkly as she comes past—like a strange breeze she moves past—and he knows now that maybe he is scared a little of button-pretty Sue.

So where'd you hook up with this lot then?

One minute I'm at Saint Hilary's, she says.

Saint fucking Hilary's?

And the next? I've met this bloke on the train.

Blokes on trains? Never a good idea, sweetheart.

Turns out he's Joe Director.

Love and fate, he says.

Why's it you're here really? she says.

I've been indignantly asking myself that same fucking question, Sue.

From above there is a mighty hog's bark—the Amethyst is not good on the nerves—as Joe Director goes hard, hard at the boy Frank, and he can hear Frank's sputtering, and he can hear his cries.

You think this stuff gets you places, Sue?

You leave it inside it poisons and twists.

That's what I used to think.

Used to?

He turns an eye in to meet its other—a goon-show for the daft kid—and she halfways smiles.

Where'd he really find you, this Joe?

There is an arrogance to her; it's a kind of shine—the star-of-youth—and it lights the haunts of her elfin or woodland face.

I've told you. I was always going to come here.

She goes up the stair. She looks back at him for a slow, held moment as she turns the stair. She disappears into the strange room up there. And the screeches in the room come down to sobs and groaning as her voice goes among the others, and he can hear new, fast, urgent whispers, as of love.

He sits auntishly in the comfy damp chair.

Next, a great manic slam and entry—

Return of Cornelius.

Never a dull moment, the Amethyst.

———

Not good, John. The pressmen are crawling like demented fucken maggots all over the province of Connaught.

Cornelius, hoarsely whispering—

I mean it's a full circus wagon of the cunts. They're camped in Mulranny. They're camped in Newport town. They're all over Westport like flies on old meat. The place is riddled with them. There's not a boat moving on the Clew that don't have a camera fixed to it. There is no earthly approach to the island at this moment in time. They could even be on the island itself . . .

Throws up the paws in a hopeless flap—

We just don't know, John.

Who sits in his armchair, cross-legged, harshly executive, with a brandy on the go, a heavy tumbler full of amber sea—

What the fuck happens now, Cornelius?

We'll need to keep you here a small while yet. And what harm?

From upstairs—

A screech.

A cry.

A Scream.

He swirls his brandy; he inclines his head towards the door.

To the garden, Cornelius. Please.

————

You've fucking landed me in it here, pal.

How so, John?

You've set me down in a freakhouse!

Ah go easy.

I want away from here and I mean now!

That could be a problem, John.

They are in conference by an old gate down the hotel's sideway. The five-bar gate sounds its hollows in the breeze. Hedges converse, it seems, the stars whisper, and the dark sea groans.

Get me the fuck out of here, Cornelius.

Through the hollow bars of the gate the breeze moves slowly to play an off-kilter tune—an arabesque.

Would you not go easy on yourself, John? For once in your fucken life?

A strange music in reverb as the breeze comes through the bars of the gate.

I've a bad feeling, Cornelius.

But that could be on account of anything at all just floating around the place. Remember you're a long way off the road when you get to the far end of Achill Island.

Meaning fucking what?

These are pure open-minded people, John.

Cornelius?

Stop. Calm yourself. And listen . . . Okay?

The breeze plays through the bars of the gate a night-song and Cornelius stands frozen there, his palm held high—

Listen?

Cornelius . . .

Do you hear, John?

The strange notes that play and turn on the air.

Maybe, he says.

That's awful sadness, isn't it, John?

But from where?

Here. Just now. Listen. And you know the funny thing about it?

What?

That feeling mightn't be your own at all.

It is a sadness that's ripe and livid on the air. He tries to hum it but he cannot—the notes will not hold or take shape.

Do you see now the way you can fall into a dream with this place easy enough if you'd like to, John?

———

I am working on a way to the island, John. We are not beaten yet. In fact an O'Grady is never beat. An O'Grady could be down on the flat of his back stuck like a pig and the guts spewing out of him like a red fucken river and he's still not beat. All I need is your patience, sweet John. Just stay hid till the place clears. Give it a day or give it two and the Clew will be clear as light. Patience is the virtue required. This is the best place for you. It's not like I can leave you with normal kinds of people. These are your own kinds of people. Just relax yourself and I'll be back again shortly. I will get you to the island, John.

––––––

A vat of goat curry simmers on the hob. It's got horn and pheromone and dark magic in. Frank stirs, Frank tastes; Frank looks a bit puzzled. Frank also is the lieutenant in charge of chickpeas.

This lot will feed the regiment, John says.

Frank has a First War face. He smiles weakly and takes up the pot of chickpeas and sets it on the drainer. He twists the end of an ashy rope of hair between a thumb and forefinger. John can see that the boy is in the room and not—his mind is all fucked with and swayed.

You've been taken apart tonight, have you, Frank?

It did get a bit thorny.

And how you doing now?

Frank sniffs at the air for a clue; he takes out a lighter and he burns the same tip of hair.

It could go either way, John.

Battle's never won, is it, Frank?

You've got one thing reckoned, he says, another comes up.

It's like laying lino, John says. Does it get violent in the room up there?

It goes 'round the edges of.

Frank tests a chickpea in his gob—he looks dumbfounded.

What exactly are you doing out here, Frank?

The boy smiles. He has milk-bottle shoulders and a North-of-England mug, that First War face.

Where's it you're from, kid?

I'm from Leeds.

A Tommy in a trench—take aim on the alleyman.

I'm sorry for your troubles, John says.

And he can see the sweet dull suburb—dad's an headmaster, isn't he?—and the sweet beaming mam; she wears a floral print; it's the better end of Leeds, this.

I want to change, Frank says.

I'm all for it, change. Every day of your fucking life you've got to change. You can't stand still, not ever. You change or you fucking die. But it's you that's got to make the change, Frank. Nobody can tell you how and nobody can show you how.

The boy narrows his eyes.

Now if I was you, Frank? I'd grab young Sue and your satchels and I'd take to the road and bloody smartish.

What gives you the right to say?

Nothing. But I look at you, Frank, and you're twenty years old or whatever you are and I think it's a shame you've got your head all mangled up by this old hog who's set himself up as some kind of fucking guru out here, some kind . . .

No leaders here.

Oh look around you, Frank. Open your dim fucking eyes.

But the boy just shakes his head in sadness and covers the chickpeas with a tea towel.

Grub soon, he says, and leaves the room.

High in a corner of the room a spider rides a breezeblown web and there isn't even a window open.

A hurdy-gurdy plays somewhere from a hi-fi and from elsewhere there is a dull sobbing.

Not good not good not good.

———

By night he'll creep in on tiptoes to watch the child sleeping. There is something in the way that he breathes that stops all the time inside. A trace of slime above his lips—a snail's slime, a silver—and John wipes it clean with an edge of his T-shirt softly as he can so's not to wake him. The city outside quiet as it ever can be. The black breathing of the park. And the way the past is dropping away. He stays as quiet as he can, he hardly takes a breath—at last the past is dropping away—and the kid unglues an eye—so silently—and has a peep and he takes him up to love and they stand together in the blue of the night above the streets and park, and the city for half a moment is quiet as it ever can be, and they are blue in love and doomed in all the usual ways.

———

Joe Director pads softly across the lobby in his flowing garb. He positively fucking wafts across the lobby. He has a little Moroccan teapot held daintily in the one paw and a small cine camera in the other. He'll want to watch himself with that fucking camera. He sighs even as he walks, and there is something that changes on the air as he comes across. He has an odd weight on the air, as a ghost has weight.

John-kid, he says. A toppener?

We will sit over our nettle tea together. There is no want out the Amethyst Hotel for nettle fucking tea. We will sit and primly sip our tea in this spell of midnight pleasantness. Joe Director stretches and yawns; he lifts his fat little feet and he kicks them out into the air for a bit and he lets them drop again, wearily.

You're tired, Joe?

Wall-fallin', he says.

John can feel his stomach contract. There is something in the tone or note. There is something in the waddling Northern vowels. There is something off. We will sit parked in the lobby like a pair of very deranged guests. Joe places the camera significantly on the floor between them and slowly now he tells a version of himself. He tells of all the mad sisters and all the feral brothers, all packed together like ferrets in a sack, and this was in a nothing house, and this was on a nothing street, and this was under the coalsmoke and Lancashire sky and

—nettle tea, a careful sip; on he drones—

the rancid squats in London town—someplace horrid, wasn't it Ealing?—and the camp in Spain, and the dogs and the junk and the lizard women, and the babies with stars for eyes

—I beg your pardon, Joe?—

and a black-sand beach for a winter—all the junk—and a lost-time in Morocco—medina whispers—and if any of it is true or not, John does not care, all he wants is to hear the telling, having an interest, as he does, in such arrogant freaks.

We are what we pretend to be, aren't we, Joe? For a finish?

He does not like this—his smile is thin, grey, cattish.

You've been out here for a while have you, Joe?

Been here for years now.

The smile warms; there's a flip of the wrist.

Feels like nothing, he says. So long as you're keeping busy.

You know about my island, Joe?

I knew some of the people you had on it for a bit.

The Diggers?

Same as.

I heard there was a fire out there.

I heard as much, John.

He takes out a lighter and wraps a wiry strand of his hair around a fat thumb; he sets fire to the end of the strand.

The high note of its bitter scent flashes on the air.

Joe?

He takes up the camera, and trains it, and sets it with a flick of the thumb to its whirring.

No thanks, John says—he raises a palm against it.

Not even a quick hello, John?

Put the fucking thing down.

————

And might it be out there still—or up there—somewhere, in an old freak's effects, or on the spidering web, just a few seconds at the end of a reel as the tall man, gaunt with tiredness, holds a palm against the lens and pushes it away firmly, angrily, and the hog-like man chuckles, and it is past midnight at the Amethyst Hotel—are there witches moving on the beach?—and all the stars are out, and Mars is a dull fire in the eastern sky.

————

They settle again to their sipping; they settle again to their talk.

I've had some luck in my life, John. I've had an angel's share. But for you to show up at our little place here? Well that's something very special indeed.

There's an arrogance to him, and the hoggish smile, and the query comes now just as expected—

Do you want to come up the room, John?

He says—

Joe?

Yeah?

Have you any idea how long it'll be before Cornelius gets back?

———

Sometimes he'll walk the streets on the biblical afternoons when a great downpour hits the avenues and it rains frogs and cats and dogs and the people all become strange twisted birds in the hot wind from the tunnels and get sucked down the black maws of the subways and the taxi cabs move through the yellow blur and vapours of the streets and the rain washes the colours of the streets and smears them and he comes down from his eyrie and walks the streets for a while and he is that happy in his old raincoat with the fisherman's hat pulled down over his eyes—the hat a yellow oilskin makes him look like a cartoon duck—and he roams for a while around the seabed of the city and he has a natter with the crustaceans—hello?—and he goes among the pools of the streets and the mad things—the hat he's had for three bucks off a Chinese dude that keeps a stall in the

park—among the crabs and the mad—he talked to a Turkish boy once who had only the one yellow snaggle tooth and
a mouth that'd been opened with a hatchet apparently and
a T-shirt that read *Galatasary*—and for a while it feels like
his very own town and place and maybe he can work again
and breathe again and write again, and not be locked to the
fucking past—that he might play again—not locked to the
past—that he can write again—not locked to the past and its
same old song—

Lah-de-dah
Lah-de-dum-dum-dah.

———

At table—

There's Frank.

There's Sue.

There's Joe Director.

It is two in the morning. It is early in the Maytime. It is a
whispery old dining room. There is a vat of goat curry and a
giant wooden bowl of spiced chickpeas with mint and parsley
and there are bottles of cold Madeiran wine. Into the grain of
the wooden table the words

B L A C K
A T L A N T I S

are carved and from a hi-fi the boozy sitars waft—a dozen years he's been trying to outrun the fucking sitars. Spoon up the curry from the antique delft. It's tasty as hell.

Kid, says Joe. Tender as such.

Drink the cold sweet wine—it's a very nice old wine. Let the night drift out a little. Get looser. The delft shows a little Dutch kid. The finger-in-the-dyke kid. What's-his-face? Outside the pale night is stretched across the sky.

Black Atlantis, Joe?

Joe Director nods sombrely.

It's outside the window, John.

Joe Director is a forest hog.

Frank is a wolf.

Sue, an elf.

And John?

I have made my own shell—

I am the clam,
the barnacle,
the brittlestar.

———

Do you want to come up the room, John?

No, I don't.

Do you want to get the rants on, John?

No, I fucking don't actually because what I realise right now I'm sat here is I don't need to scream no more and I don't need to rant neither because I know who I am and what I am and what I am is I'm a full-grown fucking man. I don't need to do that stuff anymore.

Come on, John . . .

Look, he says. After a while you've gone and opened yourself up plenty. And you can just let it fucking lie. But you lot do whatever you need to do to get yourselves through the night. Don't let me stop you.

You want to make a circle, John?

I'm good but thanks.

You want to get the rants on, John?

I've said no! I don't want to get the fucking rants on!

Do nothing you don't want to do, John-kid.

Well that's just fucking fine then.

———

He drinks a bit and smokes a bit and drifts. The light of the moon comes through in witchy rays. He thinks—

What if we were to run away for real? Say to Buenos Aires to a secret compound behind high gates with Hector on security detail with his machine gun and his 'tache. Or make it a tiny fiefdom in a jungle someplace—a Kurtz. Or make for the desert. Or what about Berlin in an old factory packed with hypodermic flunkies. Or what about Budapest. Or what about fucking Barnsley. Or say he goes upriver, or say he goes underground, or say he's a shepherd in Patagonia—of course you've got your Welsh down there, bloody Taffs, they get everywhere—or say he just clings to a rock out in the middle of the black fucking ocean

Taffy was a Welshman, Taffy was a thief

on his own tiny Atlantis

as kids we sang, on the street we sang

on his nineteen rabbity acres—or what about a fucking trout farm in Wales—do a Roger Daltrey on it—and let there be no . . .

You're on the move, John?

This is Joe Director.

You what?

You've left the room, John. You might pretend to be here but you're not. It can't contain John, the Amethyst.

Frank and Sue are quiet, smiling, watchful.

Come on up the circle, John.

Fuck off.

What about we do the rants, John?

You're a bunch of fucking throwbacks.

Come on, John.

It's 1978!

We could go up the room, John.

I'm done with all that stuff. I'm done with all that open up and bleed.

We could go to the room right now.

Come on, John, says Sue, and she's up, an elf, and she has his hand in hers, and her touch is so light.

Come on, John, says Frank, a young wolf, and he's up, and moving.

The time is now, John, says Joe Director. Let's go inside.

Part Four

THE RANTS

Pale night.

An upstairs room at the Amethyst Hotel.

Once a room for dancing, its ghosts, unseen, move in silence across the old boards still.

Sea-rasp outside hoarse as love by night whispered.

The room is bare but there are symbols of the occult daubed on the walls.

On the floor in a corner of the room a tapered candle burns on a saucer of Dutch patterned delft—the flame sputters and twists in the breeze that comes through the room and the red wax melts in beads that fall to pool and harden on the faded blue of the delft.

The symbols on the walls are in a red daubing as of blood.

The light of the candle is feeble and yellowish—the pale blue of night dominates against it.

High windows are left open to the night.

Moths in flight are shown though feebly in the throw of candle-light.

Joe, Frank, Sue and John squat upon the boards to make a Ranters' circle there.

They are an hour in, and they are already past the worst of it—

JOHN   I said shut your fucking hatch you little elf-faced fucking witch!

SUE   Oh why don't you shut your fucking beak you lying rat-faced bastard!

FRANK   Go harder, Sue.

SUE   What you are, John? You really want to know what you are?

JOHN   Oh fuck off! I mean what gives you the right? Fuck off!

SUE   What you are . . .

JOHN   On the fucking broom you rode in on!

SUE   . . . is a fucking suck machine. You're just a rich guilty bastard away on a skite. You come out here . . .

JOHN   You can do better than this, Sue.

SUE   . . . and the way you look down at us? In your arrogance? When it's you that shows up here? With your whingy
fucking snout stuck in the air and your whingy fucking beak
all twisted oh and . . .

*Hard veins of assault rise in Sue's neck; their blue pulsing is an
alien form in the room; she loudens.*

SUE   . . . it's give-to-me, give-to-me, give-to-me, that's what
you're saying, that's what you're asking, every fucking cell
you got it's screaming give-to-me, give-to-me, give-to-me—
you're a fucking leech and paranoid come calling and saying it with your eyes—suck-suck-suck—make it all easy and
calm and sweet forme . . .

FRANK   Leech come crawling.

SUE   . . . is what you're saying, fucking leech . . .

JOE   Suck the blood.

SUE   . . . and justify, justify, tell me I've done all the right
things, won't you, tell me I've let no one down not ever, won't
you, and you can't even see you're the most superior fuck
that ever stood up and all you are is a fucking . . .

Sue begins to weep.

SUE   . . . is a fucking . . .

FRANK   IS a whinging fucking hooknose bastard.

Frank Screams.

Sue rises onto her knees and makes the cocksucking gestures—cupped palm, piston wrist—and Screams and lets her eyes roll until all that shows is the whites of her eyes and she roars from her hollows at John—

SUE   Give-to-me give-to-me give-to-me! Suck suck suck suck suck! You're a fucking worm!

JOE   Harsh, Sue?

FRANK   Harsh to fucking worms.

Joe Director's hands move to his belly to bed down the chuckles there. He is a proud old hog.

Sue exhales sharply from her nose and falls to the seated position again; Sue deflates and wipes her tears away.

John raises his hands behind his head and knits his fingers there; his smile is dew-bright, amused, morning-fresh.

JOHN   You're gonna have to do better than this, kids. Much better.

Sue smiles and shakes her head—John winks at her—and now she sticks her tongue out and she loads indecency into her eyes. She lets her voice drop an octave—there is throat and smoke in it now.

SUE   I know what you fucking want.

JOHN   Oh try harder! Please! Coz I've had the real nasties thrown at me, you know. And by proper fucking maniacs.

SUE   Let's talk about cunt.

JOHN   You're too fucking obvious.

SUE   Fuck me fuck me fuck me. Is that what you want to hear, John? Let's talk about love.

JOHN   Oh behave, child.

FRANK   Here we go.

SUE   You want to have in, don't you, John?

She lays her hand on her breastbone—brittle as a bird's beneath the brocade of her blouse—and drums the tiny pads of her fingertips there.

Frank Screams.

Joe Director shakes his head and glowers. He is an angry old hog but he speaks quietly.

JOE   Now listen up. You pair? Frank and bloody Sue. You pair are sounding like you're sexually frustrated. You'd swear you've not had your bit. Have you not had your bit, Frank? Are you frustrated, Frank? I said are you?

Joe Director rises and crosses the circle and he thumps Frank hard about the side of the head; the boy whimpers and recoils.

Joe mocks the whimper; Sue mocks the whimper.

Frank rises onto his knees and shakes his head viciously at Joe and lets loose a dog snarl and weeps.

FRANK   I've had my fucking bit!

JOE   Oh? And what about you, lovely Sue?

Joe Director shimmies his hips in merriment as he pushes Frank back down with the palm of his hand to the crown of the boy's head and now he roars—

JOE   I said have you not had your fucking bit, Sue? I said have you not had your come-come, Sue? I said have you not had your fucking squirmy?

SUE   Fuck off you fat diseased prick!

Joe slaps her face.

Frank Screams.

John is thinking: Nice crowd we've in tonight.

Sue makes a sex noise—a chocolate moan.

John is thinking: They're here all week, folks.

FRANK   I think John-John needs his fucking squirmy.

JOHN   Okay! Kiddies! Hold up! Please! And fucking listen! Coz you want to know what I fucking think? I think you should all go and sign up for fucking accountancy college! I think you're a bunch of fucking throwbacks! I mean it's 1978!

FRANK   We can see your problem, John.

JOHN   Oh? Me? I've got a problem?

Joe Director sits again; his eyes blaze but he lights a smile and speaks softly—

JOE   Oh you've got a problem, John. Believe it.

A silence holds for a slow beat.

The air feels restricted now—the room feels tight as a drum.

The night aches a slow moment beyond the high windows: it is Achill Island in the Maytime of 1978.

Streaks of nightgreen, iridescent, work the ribs of the water beneath.

Mountains lie in silhouette against the pale sky.

Somewhere a blackbird sings.

And now, unseen by the Ranters, a thumbprint appears in the pool of hardening wax on the Dutch patterned saucer.

John speaks coldly—

JOHN   I really don't think you're up to this. In fact I think you're a bunch of rank fucking amateurs. I think you're working from a manual. I don't think there's any way you're gonna break through here. I mean absolutely fucking no-how. Coz my old skin? I've got a skin on it's like a leather fucking hide.

A breeze moves through the bare room again; there are sighs of sea.

JOE   And nothing beneath, John?

SUE   Nah, he's just a fucking . . .

Sue bites on her lip as she searches out the word.

SUE   Vacancy.

She closes her eyes—John feels a chill, a touch—and now her words come rabidly, super-quick, in a machine-drone:

SUE   There's nothing there, John, except the fear, all the fear you got in, we can all see the fear you got in, it's everything about you is the fear and we can smell it, the fear and . . .

The veins of her neck rise to pulse in blue again.

SUE   . . . all you want is others to give, give, give and justify all you've fucking done and said and you want us to say oh

John, John, all your choices were the right choices, John, and you didn't want to hurt nobody never but the truth is you're a fucking sellout, John, and you're a liar, John, and you're just suck-suck-suck, it's everybody else's energy you feed on, John . . .

JOHN You'll not break through here.

SUE . . . you're just suck-suck-suck and you've let everyone down who believed in you ever and you're that fucking over and you're that fucking irrelevant and what you are, John-John . . .

FRANK Is you're a whinging fucking wormbag, John.

Sue lets loose a Scream that shudders her rib cage under the slim fit of brocade; Joe Director nods in grim approval.

JOE From your sex is that, Sue-child.

Joe Director starts to play a motor growl on his lips, and he builds it to a great thrumming of sound, and a new rhythm is made, and John turns his eyes in, one to meet the other, in derision of a throwback scene; it's nineteen seventy fucking eight.

JOHN Though it passes an evening, I suppose.

Sue rises, and she weeps again as she crosses the circle—the sound of her unwellness—and she roars hard into John's face:

SUE You're nothing but a fucking . . .

but John's face is unmoved, thin-lipped, a sark.

JOHN   I know. A vacancy. You've said.

Sue makes as though to spit at him but she does not spit; she retreats and sits again.

JOHN   And maybe you're not wrong, love.

Joe Director rocks back and forth on his heels; he looks gently at John. Sympathy coats his words like honey:

JOE   You lost your mam, didn't you, John?

JOHN   Oh here we fucking go.

JOE   It must have been a very significant event in your life. You've talked about it a great deal.

JOHN   I was playing on sentiment actually, Joe. I was taking the piss out of popular fucking sentiment. Coz it's like fucking junk. It's fucking sedative. It holds you back and it keeps you down.

Tiny synapse burn of a moth's wing singed by candle flame—a protein hiss.

JOE   They said she liked the blokes, your mam? That must have been very hurtful, John.

JOHN   You think I give a flying fuck about the crap that gets printed in crappy fucking papers, Joe?

JOE   It must be very distressing, John. The intrusion.

JOHN   You think I give a flying fucking toss about the *News of the* fucking *World*?

JOE   How did it make you feel, John?

JOHN   I know where I stand with them, Joe. I know who I fucking am. I know what'll be thrown at me by fucking pigs with fucking typewriters.

Joe Director shows a palm and shushes.

JOE   We're just trying to peel that skin back, John. Relax yourself.

JOHN   I'm utterly fucking relaxed. Trust me.

JOE   In that case . . .

Joe gestures to Sue.

John's heart beats quick and hard like a trapped bird's.

Sue rises and crosses the circle and stands glowering at John.

Joe Director slaps the floor.

JOE   Now have in, Sue!

She lays a palm softly to John's face—he shucks free of it.

JOE   Do you not like to be touched, John?

JOHN   Fuck the fuck off!

FRANK   Have in, Sue.

Sue strokes John's neck with the petals of her fingers. They are that soft. A chill cuts through him again—he can feel the odd vibrations the girl is charged on; they are of the woodland places; she is elfin; in her fingers fused and pulsing the greens of England.

JOHN   Actually you're tripping me the fuck out here, love.

Wind-rasp; sea-sigh.

And Sue runs lightly a thumbnail across his lips.

JOHN   I said would you please mind fucking the fuck off, love?

But she leans in closer still and aims a lover's breath to the side of his neck—breath-of-sea—and she smells of chamomile, green youth, base cocaine.

JOE   Have in, Sue.

FRANK   Have in, John.

JOE   Where did shy ever get you, John-kid? Fuck the little witch.

She comes closer again. She makes to kiss John—the un-shy poke of her tongue emerges—but John rises—John's up—and he paces fast on the Amethyst boards.

JOHN   I said fuck off!

But Sue follows him, walking swankily, with her palms laid on her tiny hips, all lady-like—Lady Godiva, a swagger and sway— but it's in mockery of him.

JOHN   I said behave and back the fuck off, witch!

SUE   Say you don't want to do me, John.

JOHN   Oh come on, love! I could be your fucking dad!

SUE   What are you scared of?

JOHN   Ten types of fucking gonorrhoea!

JOE   Leave him be and sit for now, Sue.

Sue pouts and blows a raspberry taunt; she retreats and sits; her neat chin juts saucily; Lady Godiva.

JOE   I think we need to remember that John suffers. Let's remember that he's a great man is John. Let's not forget. He's made a big difference has John. With his little TV appearances. With his little wafty speeches and his fucking chants and . . .

John shakes his head and smiles. He drifts to the corner of the room where the candle burns; he looks at the flame and on the saucer of delft the hardening beads of wax—there is a thumbprint in the wax.

JOHN   Here we fucking go.

John walks back to the circle and sits again; he smiles—it's as though he can take it.

JOE   . . . his hatred for his own self and all that he's made of because he's nothing now, not anymore he's not, he's just a fucking richman worm . . .

Joe closes his eyes to make the words: Joe Director is charismatic, hog-fat, dark-as-fuck.

JOE   . . . a spawky fucking Irish peasant worm with his new money and his faggot hands and . . .

JOHN   Oh fuck off!

SUE   We're getting closer.

JOE   . . . his fear, all the fear he's got in . . .

JOHN   Oh fuck off you fat fucking goon!

FRANK   Truth is cruel, John.

JOE   Is that a little colour in your cheeks, John?

JOHN   You don't fucking know me!

John rises again and he moves towards Joe Director, and now Frank lets loose a Scream, and now Sue thumps the floor with her palms, and Screams.

JOHN   You don't know the first fucking thing about me! I said not the first thing! You want to remember I've been down this road many fucking times. I've spent months going at myself and bloody hard and with the fucking best of them. I've been harder on myself than anyone else could ever fucking be! I've sat with Dr. Janov him fucking self. He was my friend! In California . . .

Sue stretches the word, a mockery of him—

SUE   Cali-fo-nee-yah!

JOHN   And you can fuck off and all with your daft fucking tits and your daft elfy fucking eyes!

JOE   Have a go, Frank.

Now Frank rises—Frank's up—and he comes close to John; they are face-to-face, chest-to-chest.

JOHN   Oh back off, child!

JOE   Go, Frank.

The boy shimmers with the threat of violence.

FRANK   You're just a whinging fucking bitch!

SUE   Tell him, Frank!

JOE   Be a fucking man, John! Stand up!

John pushes Frank hard at the chest and he screeches at the boy and Frank stumbles back, and now he retreats, and sits again; he smiles.

John breathes hard—with his hands on his hips—and he looks at them.

The way they stare back at him, smugly, expectant, amused: a family of three.

Outside, the waves' slow boom and collapse.

Something gives.

JOHN   Do you really want to know what I am? Do you? Well I'll tell you exactly what I fucking am. I'm fucking anxiety. And I'm fucking lust. And I'm a fucking booze hound and I'm a fucking dope fiend or I was and I'm a fucking sad Scouse sentimental bastard and I'm the most competitive prick on the face of the planet actually and I'm a jealous greedy black-hearted English cunt full of bitterness and fucking poison and fucking rage and I'm the sweetest fucking angel, too, while we're fucking here and while we're fucking at it or at least sometimes I am and that is who I fucking am and that is what I fucking am and yeah I miss me dead fucking mam and yeah I want to piss on me dead fucking dad's fucking bones coz he didn't fuck her enough and he didn't make her fucking happy and you know what that makes me?

A delighted silence—three breaths are held.

JOHN   It makes me fucking special fucking no-how!

JOE   Exceptional, John.

JOHN   Me dead fucking dad? I tell you now I want to go down to fucking Brighton or wherever that twat's laid to rot . . .

JOE   Oh this is very nice.

JOHN   . . . and I want to scrape his peasant fucking eyes or what's left of 'em from the sockets of his skeleton head and tear his fucking bones apart with me fucking teeth or what's left of his fucking bones . . .

JOE   I'd suggest more of this, John. Plenty more.

JOHN   . . . and yeah, you're right, Joe, I can't get over what I've fucking come from and I . . .

JOE   Would you like to burn off some base, John?

JOHN   No, I fucking wouldn't coz I don't do that no more and I don't do fucking junk neither and I don't hardly drink

neither! Coz I'm a good little boy who bakes the bread and
has a fag and minds the kid and minds his business and
minds his own fucking yard.

JOE   Do you get sour thoughts often, John?

John goes to the window—

He leans out and tries to suck all the air from the night.

He feels a breath on his neck but it cannot be.

He opens his mouth to Scream but he cannot.

He turns back to the circle: a family of three.

*Sue turns her hands to display on the insides of her wrists the raw
scars and the welts there.*

Frank Screams.

*John is thinking: What the fuck is this exactly some suicide fuck-
ing death cult fucking caper?*

And Sue Screams so hard she brings a green bile up.

JOE   That's a useful effort is that, Sue.

*The Barnsley or the Blackburn of him; the Lancaster busman of
him; and Sue rises—Sue's up—and she goes to the window and
spits all the bile and spew away.*

The birds outside fall silent as the night thickens.

Sue returns to the circle. She is placid again. John watches her carefully as she sits down on the boards.

Now John returns to the circle and sits, too.

He is worn, pale, drawn, opened.

JOE   Let's talk some more about your mam, John.

JOHN   Oh come on. I mean, please. I'm thirty-seven years old. I'm fully fucking grown. Do I really need to yodel on about me dead fucking mam and me dead fucking dad all the time? Is it not enough that I live back there half the time? Back in nineteen thirty what-fucking-ever? Can I not just get on with my life now?

A sally of breeze comes through the room; the flame of the candle wavers and rights again.

Joe Director speaks but softly—

JOE   Why don't you tell something about them, John?

JOHN   Oh, I see. We've moved on to the tender bit, have we?

JOE   Well why not?

Joe Director works the quietness that settles on the room.

He holds John's gaze and loads trust on the line that runs between them—the weight takes and holds.

JOE   What's to be afraid of, John?

Frank's head falls onto Sue's shoulder and with her fingertips she touches his face and he shudders.

SUE   Oh come on, John.

FRANK   Tell us something, John.

The silence holds for a slow beat; then—

JOHN   Are you lot for fucking real?

JOE   You know that we are. Come on, John.

JOHN   Oh fuck off.

JOE   Come on.

JOHN   You're really serious?

JOE   Come on.

Something gives; the room lightens; John deflates.

JOHN   What kind of fucking thing?

JOE   First thing comes to mind.

JOHN   About them?

JOE   Yes.

JOHN   I don't fucking know.

JOE   Anything? First thing?

JOHN   They were tiny.

JOE   Oh?

And John is in the drag of the past.

JOHN   He must have been what? Five foot bloody three or something. Coz he'd worn leg braces as a kid. He was a regular fucking gimp arse. Fucking Freddie. And she was smaller again.

JOE   A neat little pair. Where's it they meet?

JOHN   This I know . . . It was Sefton Park.

JOE   A roll in the bushes?

JOHN   I don't fucking know, do I? I mean whatever you weren't supposed to do, that's what she'd go and do . . . They were excitable little people, my mam and dad.

JOE   Excitable how?

JOHN   They'd get carried away on a notion. They'd make lots of fucking plans. They were daft bloody schemers.

JOE   Kind of plans?

JOHN   They were going to open a pub together. Or was it a café? There'd be music and dancing and all sorts. It would go on all night. Some kind of bloody cabaret was the notion.

JOE   Tell about him.

JOHN   He's from Irish. He's got left in the Bluecoats like a fucking orphan. I could do you the violin.

JOE   Why's it his mark's on you still?

JOHN   How should I know?

JOE   Why's it both their marks on?

JOHN   How should I fucking know? Coz they played the fucking banjo?

JOE   The fucking . . .

JOHN   Banjo. I know! The pair of 'em played fucking banjos.

Joe   Bloody hell. And did they sing?

JOHN   She'd do her Vera Lynn. He'd do his Al Jolson.

The vaudeville halls; the North-of-England. The Lancashire-Irish. The pug faces. The waft of sick and ale. The fagsmoke. The sawdust. The smell of piss and chips.

JOE   What happened to them?

JOHN   I don't know. Whatever it is that happens to people.

JOE   She fucked around on him?

JOHN   You've been reading the nasty papers, Joe. Tinpot guru sat on Achill Island with his *Daily Mirror* and his bag of shite cocaine cut with fucking rat poison.

JOE   She's fucked around on him, John?

JOHN   Oh I don't fucking know, do I? And I mean who cares? I mean everybody's fucked everybody else by now, haven't they? I mean it's 1978!

JOE   Was he jealous of her?

JOHN   I don't fucking know. He'd went away, hadn't he?

JOE   He'd went where?

JOHN   He'd went to sea. Where else do they bloody go? Merchant fucking seaman.

His voice is tired and hollow.

The candle spits and gutters.

JOE   Did you hate her for fucking about? Or hate him for taking off?

JOHN   Oh who cares anymore? It's dead history! And what can people do about them-fucking-selves? In the end? I mean it's the fucking blood and it's fucking fate and it's all laid down in advance.

JOE   There's Irish.

JOHN   And there's no fucking escape.

JOE   There's very Irish. How'd they mark you, John?

JOHN   They made me choose between them.

JOE Director watches carefully the moment—he weighs it in his graven palm.

JOE   Why are you here, John?

John rises and goes to the window and looks out . . .

JOE   What are you hiding from, John?

. . . to the oblivious sea that holds in its palm the island of Achill and the sky with . . .

JOE   What are you scared of, John?

. . . its first fade in the east. He turns and looks at them coldly now.

JOHN   I can see how you operate out here, Joe. You just take these daft fucking kids and play with their fuck juices, don't you? You put your daft thoughts in their daft fucking heads and in their daft fucking bits and it's all too easy, isn't it, Joe?

JOE   And what's it you've been up to for twenty years?

JOHN   You're just a fucking user. It's all too easy, Joe. Too easy to make it a little kingdom out here and you're the fucking despot and you're king of the heap with your cocaine and your daft fucking clobber and I couldn't care less what you've been up to in the Amethyst fucking Hotel . . .

JOE   This is a paranoid thought pattern, John.

JOHN   . . . coz I'm here to tell you what you fucking are, pal, and what you are is a pig. You're going to die and rot and no one'll give a fucking toss anyhow. Maybe these two fucking halfwits have some hope. Maybe they're young enough . . .

HE starts to walk from the room.

JOE   John-kid?

JOHN   I need to sleep.

SUE   It's not too late, John.

JOHN   I want to know as soon as Cornelius gets back.

FRANK   Did you know that Mars is about, John?

———

He goes to the room marked nine. He closes the door after. He sits on the bare mattress. The world takes its shapes outside but greyly. He can hear their voices down the hallway still.

By the breath of the sea the morning comes closer. He becomes certain that he is in danger. It will be too late to move once the brightness comes through.

He lies on the bed and tries to swat the fear away but cannot and he listens and after a while the voices come nearer but fade again.

A quietness settles—is it the sound of their waiting?

He lies in the stew of his fear and sour thoughts.

He lies almost without breathing—are there voices again?

He waits until a true silence holds about the old hotel and he rises from the bed and goes to the door and opens it by the inch and the inch again—there are no voices—and he moves along the hallway, so quietly, and he hardly takes a breath as he moves—no voices, no footsteps—and he comes down the stair and through the lobby and he walks out of the Amethyst and into the world.

Part Five

BLACK ATLANTIS

He sits in the cave. He listens for their voices but all he can hear is the slow release of the sea—a dissolve, or hissing. His mind is on the blink. His heart pumps the fear. His lips make words madly. Words that are set to run backwards. Words that run off in all directions. He has a set of nerves on like a sack of fucking snakes. He names himself backwards—Nhoj. A Bedouin in a tent? Under the starry cold desert sky. He sits in the cave. He listens very hard but there are no voices. He is way off the beam now. He is a fucking halfwit for even thinking he could walk out in the world still.

Outside, the sea moves. There is a foul hypnosis to it. There is a terrible queasiness to it. Vast creatures moan in the sea's great room. He listens so hard that his tongue lolls. There is a new, odd, unlovely music on his brain—

He can hear squalling accordions and the manic trembles of timpani.

He can hear the white noise of a migraine feedback.

He can hear madhouse screeches and sawblade whines.

Well I'm in some kind of hell out here, aren't I?

He tries to slow each breath as it passes through. He is scared but lit by a strange excitement, also. He feels that he is close to the edge of something new.

That gull's cry sounds just like a lost child mewling.

———

He hides all day in the cave. He has put down some difficult days in his time and here's another for the fucking annals. It is the movement of the water that works after a long while to calm him. There is an aching sound deep down in the rocks. He hears it as something close to a human sound.

He listens for their voices. The night creeps into the cave like a quiet animal—there are no voices.

Half-dark the May night cloaks the island again and the sea—he is so very far from home and love.

A fish jumps to break the surface of the water and his heart pops loose of its box and the fish is gone again but he is alive on the silver of its skin.

There is an opening-up inside. His mind turns again on its rusty old motors. Despite it fucking all. He feels that giddiness and he feels that grandeur.

An elegant, a dark gothical seabird appears and moves its slow-beat-steady wings across and just inches above the water.

First streaks of nightgreen run the sky.

Nobody can find him out here. He is safe here for a while at least. He digs his monkey toes into the sand and feels the tiny grains as they roll the crevices of the skin and slowed by his clamminess they cake. There have been other animals in this cave before. There have been other animals among these rocks before. He can feel them here still. In the sand deeply buried their chalk-white and brittle bones—

Elkbone.

Wolfbone.

Sealbone.

The words bring a dark turn. How might it be never to leave this place? To open a vein into the fine white sand. His lips sting hard with salt as though he's had a feed of chips. The rocks pitch their aching—maybe he will never escape this place—and the way the oil and vinegar soak the brown paper of the bag to translucence.

Blow a ring of the breath on each chip to cool it off—

Hoff!

The hunger pang tells him that he is alive and not for leaving.

The slivers of an odd tune come right inside—it sounds like it comes from the future, or else it comes from deep in the past.

The slivers fade as quick but what you do is you just wait—

Slowtime; cavetime; the silver of the sea-night.

_____

Sometimes when his nerves are in rags it does some good to recite the numbers of the Liverpool buses—

The sixteen for Princes Park.

The forty-two for Mount Vernon and Edge Hill.

The seventeen—Kirkdale; the nine—Dingle.

Buses for Crosby, Walton, Anfield Road, and the rainsome air and the steam of a caff—an egg and chip, a mug of tea you'd walk your boots across—and the yellow of the yellow of the egg yolks—so queasy and vibrant—and the long flirtations over frothy coffees—it's from a good convent you get the better quim, the cheeky skirt, the turned-up noses and try-me eyes—and as he dreams his heart begins to slow again, and ease.

Cavetime.

He opens his eyes. He watches over the water. He listens carefully in the gaps between the wind. There is never a silence on the island that is true. There is always something that is out there, and moving.

———

He stands in the dark vault of the cave.

The night sea gleams; it moves its lights in a black glister.

The water drags the shingle and the sound is slow and luxurious—

an old king in silverbeard fans a palmful of gold coins to a table-top covered with white cloth

—and the rocks ache and he sighs in agreement with them. It has never been easy nor was it meant to be.

The fine sand of the cave's floor comes up to a brilliant white in the moon's glow. His skin is so white in the glow. He has been ever such a whiteman always—ever the honky, ever the goy.

There is a hard splash as the water splits, and the great sleek head shows, and the dapper spindles of the moustache, and the long fat body works its muscles onto the rocks.

It sidles up to the cave's entry—hello?—and pokes a sober look inside.

The sad doleful eyes; the night caller; the seal.

There is a moment of sweet calm as their eyes lock on each other's.

Alright? he says.

Alright, John, the seal says.

———

And I'll tell you another thing.

Go on?

All this . . .

He swings his head to indicate the world beyond—he's got a fat stern head on like a bouncer.

Fucked, he says.

You don't mean . . .

I do, John. It won't last.

You mean everything?

The works, he says.

But it sounds as *wehrks*.

The wind, the waves, the water, he says.

But it sounded as *wawteh*.

It's all in extra time, he says. It's all of it fucked, son.

Mostly what John cannot get his head around is the Scouse accent.

So where's it you're from originally?

You'd know Formby way, John?

Would I? Half my bloody life out there as a kid.

Bunkin' off, was it?

Now you have me.

————

In a cold sun—wintertime—with their coats laid down in a hollow of the dunes, a salt-lipped girlie, and the way that he kissed her and got a throb on, and he kissed her and put his hand between her legs—*clamp*. The sudden military clench-ing of her thighs.

John?

It's fine.

Don't.

I won't then.

The magic words—she opened her legs—and it happened for a while but not for long, and there was the train home—through grim Bootle—and the searching for words—the Albert Dock—and the shifting in seats—Central station—can I see you the Wednesday then?—maybe, I don't know—and the blue suburbs—maybe, I don't think so, John—and aunt and home, the home that was his only home.

————

You can't go back, John.

But I just been.

He eyes the seal hard. He wants some fucking answers here. He has come all this way.

Let me see if I can explain things, John. What you do is you open your eyes in the morning, okay? First thing? And it's a particular world that appears . . . Am I right?

Yeah?

And what it's got is . . .

is the fall of black hair on the white of her skin

. . . the look of a world that's always been. As if it will never change, as if it will never break up, as if it will never disappear . . .

John cuts in—

I've a feeling I'm not about to hear anything good here.

The seal laughs but ruefully.

Reality, John, tends not to hang around. A lonely bloody suburb in 1955—it's gone—and the rattle of the train for Central under your bony arse—it's gone—and the smell of the sweat and the red raw of the acne and a tumble in the Formby dunes—it's gone—and her with a kisser on that tastes of salt and Bovril . . .

He hadn't remembered the Bovril tang—a strange seal this.

. . . and all of it, John? It's all got the same weight as a bloody dream.

So what's left that's real?

This, the seal says. Where you're sat just now.

The clouds drift to hide the moon; the cave darkens. A pool of silence is allowed to open. The silence is a tease. The seal holds it for a long while, then—

What's it you want to know?

John sits up a little straighter. He feels his mouth dry out. His words come small and shyly—

Do the, ah . . .

Go on?

Do the dead ones get together out there?

You're an odd fish, John.

I know that.

Do you mean on the water?

I think I do, yeah.

It's complicated, the seal says.

Silence—a heavy beat.

Then—

Deathhauntedness, the seal says.

Okay.

That's our little problem, isn't it, John?

John's head swings low—his remorse.

Deathhauntedness, the seal says. The fear that it's all going
to end and the measuring out of the time that's left or might
be and the morbid fear of numbers and dates and the fear of

photographs because they hold the moment in such a sad way and the sense of summer and life as a painful place, as if it's a painful place to be, out here, in life, and the fear of brightness and the fear of light and the fear of losing her, of dying first—who dies first?—and every time you hold her it's what you think—who dies first?—and the cold cold feeling that comes in the small hours

—am I getting close in yet, John? Am I getting close in yet, old pal?—

and the stewing in the past and the sense of every time being maybe the last time and everything is charged and everything glows and the night terrors that come in a soak of sweat

—you could call all of this more plainly love—

and the sentiment and the fear and the poison and the pain . . .

Don't forget the fucking isolation, pal!

I could hardly forget that, John. The sense that life is for everyone else but not for you? And you know the scariest of the lot? The very worst of it all?

Stop.

You think it might be the sweetest feeling, don't you, John?

You want to take the pain away.

You want to take the numbness away.

You want to let it fade away.

Let it fade, he says.

And he is alone then in the cave.

———

The next fucking development—

He tries to step from the cave but the white sand rises and circles its grains, slowly at first, but then faster and faster again until it's a great spinning wheel of blurred light and he's trapped inside.

He tries to Scream but nothing comes.

He cannot hear himself breathe—is he even breathing?

He cannot hear his heart beat—is it even beating?

He tries to Scream but nothing comes.

He is flung back by a great force.

The grains of sand settle again to the cave floor and for a moment a dead silence holds.

Then he hears his name called—

Joh-hhhnn?

———

The voice is taken by the wind again.

He sits in the cave and asks his heart to settle.

As if it has ever yet settled.

He watches over the water. He works to slow his breath. He sits as still as he can. The vaulted eaves of the cave contain all that's left of him.

These haunted, vaulted eaves.

He begins to gain the control of his thoughts again. He sees that the morning will come up clear. He begins to trace out the lines of something new. He says the words aloud until they come in forms and pattern. He can see the tiny detail and he can see the broader sweep.

He stands and paces between the cave's walls. He slaps a palm off each of the walls in turn, and he counts aloud as he slaps and paces, he counts from one to nine and back again.

It will contain nine songs—the nine.

He can hear the tiny fragments—he can hear the broader sweep.

There is an autumn and a winter and a cold, cold spring pouring through him now—he needs to keep pace with the rush.

It will contain nine fucking songs, and it will fucking cohere, and it will be the greatest fucking thing he will ever fucking do.

Now in the cave he has all of its words and all of its noise and all of its squall.

He sees the broad sweep—he sees the tiny detail. This is the one that will settle every score. This is pure expression of scorched ego and burning soul.

The title comes through with first light. He makes carefully with a finger the letters of the word in the white sand

beatlebone

and this is what he knows for sure:

Heard once it will haunt you fucking always.

————

The morning comes higher to make a bone-white sky. It takes away his manic joy and slips the anxiety back in. Because this is how it fucking is and this is how it fucking goes.

He is so tired. He hasn't slept a wink. He has tried so hard this long while to be at home in the world. Baking the bread. Swinging in a papoose the baby. Cosy-as-the-fucking-womb stuff. Captain fucking Domestic. Doing all the voices. Doing down the days. But his mind will go to other places. He cannot hold the moment. It is the moment itself that contains all riches. Maybe on his own island he will finally learn to hold the moment. He needs to get to his own island. He has been drawn there again for a reason. He is on the wrong fucking island. He needs to make the trip whole now.

He stands and shakes out his limbs.

Alright then, he says.

He tastes the sea and the salt, the sexiness, the early morning air.

He steps from the cave.

———

They'll call it another crack-up album. Fucking press. Fucking pigs with typewriters. Fucking typing with their fucking toes. Tappety-fucking-tap-tap. With their stubby little piggie fucking toes and their fags in their piggie little gobs and their fat little mugs of honey-brown ale. Feed their fat fucking faces. Fat typing piggie bastards.

Well, okay: crack-up album is just fine with him—

Where it all breaks loose.

Where it all comes down.

Where he breaks the fucking line.

He wants to break the line and he wants to sing his black fucking heart out and speak at last his own true mind.

World be wary, world be brave: John's about.

He walks, and he is so brave now, and he no longer listens for the voices—if the Amethyst throwbacks come at him he will rip their fucking eyes out and piss in the sockets.

He walks—

Clew Bay is laid out before him in the morning sun.

Clew Bay is where paranoia comes true.

————

He has a natter with the gulls. He explains the benefits of capitalism. He has a little sing. He finds that he has a throb on, of all things, and he'd fuck anything now, he'd fuck a clump of seaweed. He feels brave and guided; he feels clairvoyant and strong. He stops up—he's had a *stunning* thought. Is there such a thing, he wants to know, as a positive crack-up? Where the mind breaks down and re-forms again but only to show the world more clearly than before. A mind left calm as a settled pool.

Now he has a spring in his monkey step.

The sun bleeds gold from the water.

———

He kicks off his dead sneakers. Fuck you, pal, and fuck you, too. Now his feet are cut by the stones as he walks, and he bleeds, and it isn't too much of a stretch from here to a bleeding Jesus, is it?

All he needs the cross for his back.

All he needs the tears in the garden.

The tiny islands are beaded through the fields of Clew Bay. His is down there, somewhere: a fortress in the sea. All he needs is a boat to bring him to his island.

With every step he turns up another version of himself.

He walks on.

The past seeps again—the past is hidden on the dark side of every moment, just there—and it takes him to Achill when they came before; it's nine years since.

———

They walked for a while on the beach. They scrambled over the rocks. The last of the summer day was down the rockpools in its colours. There were tiny carnivals down there.

They sat for a while but it was chilly; they wouldn't sit for long. He took her hand and showed his palm and he ran the tip of her finger along the lines of his palm.

Go on, he said. What's it you see there?

They went across the rocks and heard a screeching. He took it for a squall of birds. But he saw the figures on the tideline then.

They stayed hidden among the rocks. They looked on down the beach. There were shades on the tideline. There were some women there. He counted—there were nine of them, but they were bunched together and moving as one, and they were dressed in black and as though from a faraway time.

The fuck? he said.

The women went among the waves, and they watched—rapt—as the women's screams bled out the sky, and the women kept walking until they were hip-high, until they were chest-high, until the waves broke on their pale white throats—there were nine of them in a line, their heads leant back—

Jesus fuck, he said.

—and their black clothes floated on the water, and their Screams came up to a high pitch, and died.

The women shook out their limbs against the sky.

They began to hiss and caw at each other.

They began to beat at each other.

Fucking hell, he said.

She put a finger to her lips—he wanted to pull away but she would not let him go.

Ghosts, she said.

————

He walks the length of the day. He walks on his blistering Jesus-type feet. He makes it onto a fucking road at last. Again the light is fading. He doesn't know east from west, south from north, land from sky, day from night. But he knows the van's growl as it turns a curve and comes at him fast and headlong and now it brakes hard.

Here's Cornelius—

the sorrowful little wave of the hand,

the humorous, the woeful eyes,

the sad rolling-down of the window.

This is madness, John, he says.

This is buck fucken madness, John, he says.

There is no call for this under the sun nor fucken stars, John, he says.

————

A word rolls slowly in his mouth—

Dumb-foun-ded.

Transmitted from who-knows-where, and John just sits there, and the van moves, and Cornelius talks sensibly as he steers—

People go strange out here, John. You wouldn't be the first and you won't be the last. This place has a bad fucken air about it.

Those people wanted to hurt me, Cornelius.

Nonsense, John. Those are lovely, warm, decent-hearted people. It was all in your mind.

The deep-boom beat and the lapping of the water; the van's spluttering motor; his wretched heart.

You're saying that I'm fucking paranoid?

Now that, John, is the man precisely.

The van moves; the road is taken.

What have you been doing, John?

I've been working, Cornelius.

How so?

By empathising with the common man and his everyday tragedies and his common fucking despair.

Where was this?

In a cave.

Now, Cornelius says, and he flaps a paw gracefully—it's as though the world entirely is at its ease.

Anyway there are developments, John.

Oh?

You see the way it is out here is that things can move slow enough for a long while. It's all slow, slow, slow. And then? Quick! Out of nowhere, John? Quick. All of a sudden things moving at a savage fucken pelt and the wind behind them.

He wants her so badly, he wants her touch so badly; he is so many miles from love and home.

I was worried about you, John. I won't tell a word of a lie. You could have gone over on an ankle. You could have gone over a fucken cliff. You could have been found at the bottom of it stone dead or halfways there. You could have been left a vegetable, John.

Cornelius?

But the time you were lost did us a power of good. Westport town is clear as day. Mulranny is clear. Newport is clear. The newspaper men have decided you were no more than an apparition. Clew Bay has been left entirely open to us. We have played this game sweet. Everything is just right for the excursion.

I think it's best now if you just get me to a fucking airport.

Nonsense, John. We are heading for the island.

Part Six

ELEVEN ELEVEN ELEVEN—DAKOTA

At eleven minutes and eleven seconds past eleven o'clock on the morning of November 11th, 2011

—11.11.11 on 11.11.11—

I stood on the corner of 72nd Street and Central Park West, by the entrance to the Dakota Building, with all the other hunched pilgrims, and it felt like the moment to begin.

It was impossible not to view the scene in a religious aspect: our bowed heads, the air of cathedral hush that pertained even within the city's yellow-mouthed honk and scurry, the gaudy memorial trinkets for sale across the street in the park. Zola wrote that the road from Lourdes is littered with crutches but not a single wooden leg: miracles, in other words, only go so far, and to feel any true connection or reverb at a site like the Dakota must be so rare as to be miraculous.

The city that morning had the feeling of late summer still. The colours had not caught fire yet in the fields across the park and the trees were almost fully in leaf. Shadows sat heavily to weight an intense, blue-skied clarity, and I drifted in a paranoid sea of numerological speculation. To search for hidden patterns in the arrangement of numbers—in ones, or in elevens, or in nines—is symptomatic of at least a mild disintegration, and I was not unaware of the fact.

I was operating at the usual deep thrum of anxiety and fretfulness. I was worried about both the feeds for my material and how I might subsequently arrange it. But the fact I was worried at least signalled that the work had begun.

I took out a pad and began to make a sketch of the scene. The building itself is a Gotham folly, with dark stones, sombre turrets and an air of bespooked Victoriana, and as I drew I tried to imagine within it occult dreams, and the view across the trees, say on the night of a spring gale, in the soak of an insomniac sweat, as the trees shake out their fearful limbs, and the green shimmers of the treetop faeries move like gasses through the dark. The fact that I am myself tuned to occult frequencies— and frankly I have come to a point in my life where this is no longer deniable—felt like half the battle, but still I had a nagging worry at the edges of my thought, and it was this:

If I was going to make *beatlebone* everything it should be, I needed to get to the island.

———

Clew Bay is a flooded valley—its many tiny islands are merely a scattered range of drumlin hills submerged at their bases by some unimaginably violent deluge. (Geology: slow,

slow, slow, and then quick.) There are certainly not, as the happy legend suggests, three hundred and sixty-five islands; perhaps there are half that number. The knuckle of Croagh Patrick, the pilgrim mountain, rises on the southside of the bay; to the north lies the Nephin range of County Mayo, which has an ominous air; if ever mountains can be said to *brood*, the Nephin mountains brood. On a lit, clear morning, Clew Bay is an infinitely beautiful place—especially if it is seen from a height above Mulranny, with a springtime light coming slantwise to pick out and give definition to the islands' shapes—but more often than not the Atlantic clouds swarm in from the west, moving like an invading force, or a slow disease, and the view is uncertain and shifts; the islands appear to come and go in the mist. Among the islands are Freaghillanluggagh and Gobfadda and Mauherillan. There is a Kid Island, a Rabbit Island, a Calf Island. Dorinish is in fact a pair of islands—Dorinish Beg and Dorinish More— linked by a rocky causeway. The local pronounciation would be closer to "Dur-nish" than "Dor-in-ish." In the 1970s and 1980s this place was known colloquially as Beatle Island.

———

I spent much of the winter watching clips from television interviews with John Lennon, mostly from American talk shows in the 1970s, and I replayed the same lines over and over again as I made rough drafts for voice and tried to get a fix on the intonation.

From our time and perspective, there is already an antique note to his phrasing and tone. There are verbal tics redolent of

1960s cool—many sentences end with a breezy "yunno?"—
but these are concurrent with words and formulations—and
a kind of pinched melody, actually, almost Larkinesque—that
sound like they come from an older England, the England of
austere lower-middle-class life in the war years and there-
after. He is suburban. He is a child of the early 1940s, and
thus the tentacles of his concern will reach for a time still further back: a shadow-time such as immediately precedes all of
our births, the time of the dead love stories, which is such a
heavy time. He is quite nasal and often defensive. There is a
haughtiness that can be almost princely but his moods are
capricious—sometimes he is very charming and funny and
light; at other times there is a darkness evident, and an impa-
tience that can bleed almost into bitterness. He can transi-
tion from fluffy to spiky very quickly, even within the course
of the same sentence. Often during these interviews he was
accompanied by Yoko Ono, who very clearly, from this distance, was the tethering fix in his life; lacking her presence,
you get the feeling that he might have unspooled altogether.

————

In the spring of 1967, an advert appeared in a London evening newspaper offering an island for sale off the west coast
of Ireland. Dorinish was owned by the Westport Harbour
Board in County Mayo. It was used mostly for its rocks, which
were harvested for ballast by the local fishing fleet. The listed
guide price was £1,700 sterling. John Lennon had for a long
while dreamed about an island place. He was shown the
advert and was taken with the notion.

The cliffs of Dorinish rise against the Atlantic in a way that naturally provides a buttressing effect against the prevailing winds and gives protection to the island's grasses, which retain their essential nutrients. The pasture here is perhaps the best to be had anywhere on Clew Bay and so it was that a crowd of thirty or forty interested sheep farmers were in attendance when Alistair Taylor, a trusted member of the Beatles' retinue, showed up at the auction in Westport.

It would not be difficult here to sketch a scene of comic incongruity—a beflared record company freak with hashish eyes amid the slurried ranks—and it's true that the agricultural west of Ireland in 1967 would have been a distance of decades rather than miles from psychedelic London. But in fact Taylor was short-haired, respectable, besuited, a former Liverpool docker who had worked for the late Beatles manager, Brian Epstein, and who had for a long while been trusted by the band—they called him "Mr. Fix-It."

In 1964, he had been involved with an attempt to buy Trinity Island, off the Greek coast, for all four Beatles, but the deal fell through. Just a few months before the Dorinish auction, he co-ordinated an attempt to buy the island of Leslo, also off the coast of Greece, and again for the band as a whole— the plan was that the Beatles and their familes would live on Leslo adrift from the everyday world and its dreary, nonpsychedelic concerns. A live-work-play structure, modelled on Crystal Palace, was to be built at the centre of Leslo with avenues leading from it to private quarters for each band member. This deal also fell through, but not before the band

and their wives and girlfriends visited Leslo on a chartered yacht. John and George spent the greater part of the voyage squatting on the foredeck under the influence of hallucinogens and ukuleles.

Precise details of the Westport auction have not been unearthed, and we do not know the extent of rival bids, but we know that Alistair Taylor returned to London having efficiently secured Dorinish Island for John Lennon at the knockdown price of £1,550 sterling.

————

The writer John McGahern said once that Ireland skipped the twentieth century—it went straight from the nineteenth into the twenty-first. This is almost true. The twentieth century existed in Ireland only for the half hour it took John Lennon's gypsy caravan to be sailed on a barge across Clew Bay to Dorinish Island, and the caravan is painted all the colours of the sun, and the water breaks and makes up again as the stately barge moves, and the sheets of the water spread out and come to and re-form again, and the water greys, then clears, and then colours again; it wears all the colours of the sun.

————

The sense of an ache or a wound just beneath the skin—almost impalpable but always there—is not uncommon as you move through the sobering ruts of your thirties. Psychedelic experimentation, in my own long experience, will tend to deepen or amplify this sense. Earlier, in the maelstrom rush of your twenties, in the campaign to selfhood and determination—in finding out who you are—the ache can lay buried so deeply and so quietly it might seem not to exist, but it comes back, and it has a definite weight—as though it has lain buried on the dark side of each passing moment, just there—and the urge to Scream, I believe, is by no means an unreasonable response to it.

Primal scream therapy, which is loosely grounded in Reichian philosophy, was initiated by Dr. Arthur Janov at his clinic in California in the early 1960s. Its ambition was to free the subject from the buried pain of childhood trauma. Its techniques included not just screaming but the making of a careful, guided exploration of the self and of the self's layered and shifting histories. We are each so many different versions of ourselves, after all, and the body by the passing hour can be heaven or it can be hell.

Primal scream had become a popular practice by the 1970s and especially in those places where the children of the previous decade had settled and seeded: the far-flung outposts of Aquarius. There were a number of devoted groups in Ireland, and notorious among these was a collective in Burtonport, County Donegal, on the north-western coast, who named themselves the Atlantis Community but who were more usually known, locally, as the Screamers.

———

Fictional and biographical treatments of John Lennon have tended either towards hagiography or character assassination, and I felt the wisest practice was not to do any traditional research among the texts. I did listen to the music: the Plastic Ono Band album, repeatedly—his "primal scream" record—and *The White Album*, as ever, a great deal. The voice of Alistair Taylor, incidentally, can be heard on the latter's "Revolution 9."

Above all, though, my method would be to try and spring a story from its places, from the area of Clew Bay, and Achill Island, and of course from Dorinish itself—if I could figure out how to get there—and to be guided as purely as possible by the feelings that are trapped within these places, and by the feelings trapped within.

It was on the first of my runs out west that I came across the derelict remains of the Amethyst Hotel.

———

John Lennon made his first trip to Dorinish Island in the late summer of 1967. He was ferried there by a local fisherman. He brought along a cine camera and we can see him turn on his booted heel slowly to pan and sweep up the view as the boat moves out and across the bay, as the boat's prow bites hard on the water and the slap of the low waves comes infinitely in Atlantic blacks, silvers, lichen-greens. He wears a long Afghan coat, and maybe its flapping is picked up in the camera's tinny sound recording, and the trace of voices, too—south Liverpool, the west of Ireland—but just barely, at the edges of the film, like voices at the edges of a dream.

He spent a little under two hours on the island. Snide newspaper reports would suggest that he was under the influence of LSD at the time but the estate agent involved said that in fact he was practically minded, and he made enquiries about a drainage scheme for the island. He was determined that building work should commence quickly. He had drawn a plan for a house on Dorinish—it was a fantastical house, a magic palace, as in a child's fantasy of a palace.

———

He was not alone in this migratory instinct. It had established itself quickly as a freak tradition to settle in the west of Ireland. They came from the cities to take up derelict old cottages down the ends of rainy boreens. The cottages could be had for almost nothing along the Atlantic seaboard. But it was not long, one imagines, before the idyll of a New West was smeared by the great dreariness that Ireland attempts to stay quiet about.

Imagine the near-perpetual assault of rain on a cracked windowpane, down at the shivery end of that dripping boreen—a country laneway, or a little road, dank and sodden between the whitethorn and the haw, places usually possessed in the Irish mythos by savage melancholy—with the veggie patch and the hedgerow wine, and the rising damp, and the nitty children, and the chest infections, and the freaky dogs cowering in the yard as the wind shudders their skinny flanks, and the vast hysterical skies—never light for long, never dark for long—and the low-grade hashish that burns on a slow draw, and nights of occultism, and midnight screaming, because when you live far out there's no place left to go but deep inside, and there are mean suppers by candlelight at the long tables—the endless lentils, the loaded glances, the blackberry wine—and nerves are taut as the telegraph wires that scratch against the grey sky, and there is a lot of fucking paranoia going around the freaky tables.

——————

On the way back from Dorinish, they stop off at the fisherman's house for tea and sandwiches. The fisherman has a small dog and it yaps maniacally at the hairy Afghan coat, and John is tired, and John is irked—behave, he says—but still the little dog yaps and leaps and mounts and tries to fuck his long hairy Afghan coat, and we can see the sharp nose and the green bewildered eyes, and we can hear the liquid, singular, sniping voice:

I said be-*fucking*-have!

——————

I went to Achill Island by bicycle. Sheep drifted back and forth across the road as vaguely as my thoughts moved—it was in the Maytime; I was stirred up—and my feet turned the pedals slowly into a stiff sea breeze. I didn't feel like I could reasonably ask the locals where I might find a cave. I just kept going by the nose and crab-savvy. I aimed west and then north for the island's more desolate reaches, and for an area of its coast I knew was host to a colony of seals, and near the fade of a long day—the May of 2012, clear-skied, bright, cold in the shadows still—I found just the sort of cave that I had imagined in my winter drafts.

It was precisely the correct dimensions—nine steps, east to west—and it had a floor of fine white sand, and I crawled inside and crouched there and for a long, deeply odd moment, I listened to my heart race, and it felt so familiar and true I have great difficulty believing now that I put the cave on the page before I found it on Achill.

It was my intention to spend the length of the May night there, from the last fade of light around eleven to its first return somewhere in the pale moments after four. I sat nervously and I became very anxious as true dark took over the cave. The white sand greyed, my heart beat quickly; I waited.

———

By the time of his second visit to Dorinish, in the summer of 1968, his life was in the process of being recast. The marriage to Cynthia was over, the band was halfway through the chaotic recording of *The White Album* and starting to crack, and he was in love with the artist Yoko Ono. She accompanied him on the trip. On a Saturday evening in late June, they arrived by helicopter on the lawn of the Great Southern Hotel in Mulranny. A photograph in the *Mayo News* archive shows the couple smiling on the Great Southern's lawn as they are greeted by local dignitaries.

He stayed up late to drink in the hotel bar. It was reported in the *Mayo News* that he played a tape recording of a new Beatles track called "Revolution" and announced it to the bar as the song's first public airing. The stories of this second visit are legion and the truth has by now blurred into the apocryphal. There is in particular a legend in circulation that he sang Irish rebel songs in the bar that night and that a tape recording was made of this performance.

On the Sunday there was an outing by car and road bridge to Achill Island. A picnic lunch was packed for them at a place called the Amethyst Hotel by the edge of the village of Keel. The picnic was brought into the hills to a spot with a vantage view.

I have spoken to someone who knew someone else who was on Achill that day—a day of sudden showers—and who claimed to have found in the hills an abandoned picnic site—a blanket, a hamper, wineglasses—and the sight was surreal, the way such finery was laid down amid the rocks and the gorse: the fine linen, the fine glassware, the last of the cheeses and fruit.

They went to Dorinish by helicopter. A fisherman working on Clew Bay reported that he coasted by the island and saw a figure sitting serenely on top of one of the cliffs, gazing out to sea, and another figure, lower down, clad in black, a small lady or girl, shaking her fists madly as she was divebombed by terns.

The Great Southern has since been remodelled but it retains its John-and-Yoko suite, a room no bigger or grander than any of the others but with an especially fine view of Clew Bay.

A dusty window at the Amethyst Hotel showed its derelict interior and my own face, webbed and tired, as it stared back at me. I had slept only fitfully in the cave, and I was a little wiped, and now it was a greyer May day, and the Amethyst had the feeling of a bad dream revisited. It sat at the far tip of Keel, a strung-out village with a long, beautiful beach. It had been boarded up for some time. I hunched down close to the window and peered inside. Bits of broken furniture lay about, and old phone books, and shattered crockery—there was the sense of a place evacuated at a sudden rush. The Amethyst Hotel was sinking with every moment deeper into its dereliction and fading out of time—

I went around the back and forced a door—it gave easily—and I went inside.

The hotel was built in the late 1880s by John and Eliza Barrett and named for the seam of amethyst that runs through the hills nearby. It was later owned by a Captain Robert Boyd and considered to be at the higher end of the island's accommodations. The London actor Robert Shaw owned it for a time in the 1960s and for a while it drew a louche crowd to Achill. The glamour of this incarnation did not persist. I believe I may have stayed in the hotel myself, as a child, in the summer of 1980, when we were rained off the nearby campsite.

I moved through the lobby downstairs. Clouds of dust came up as I walked by. I chanced the rickety stair. There were twenty-one bedrooms but in the final years of the Amethyst these had been turned into bedsits. I looked into some of the rooms and there were still sheets on the beds, and mummified food on the shelves. I found the room marked nine. I tried to push open the door but it caught on a scrunched wedge of damp carpet and for a moment it would not give, as if someone else stood behind the door and answered the push. But then with a quiet unearthly *whoosh* it opened, and I entered.

———

The documentary filmmaker Bob Quinn travelled to County Donegal in 1979 to record the lives and daily routines of the Atlantis Community. The resulting film, *The Family*, was considered too disturbing to be shown on Irish television, and it sat unseen for almost fifteen years, developing as it did a cult reputation.

The film shows the daily practice of the community, which revolved around primal scream therapy and furious ranted confrontations. The house itself is a large and damp-looking old seaside pile. It is painted with psychedelic swirls. There are symbols on its walls. The house ethos was to confront and to strip bare. In *The Family*, we see that this veers sometimes towards violent physical confrontation. Repression, of any sort, is taboo—the ranters let it all spill out. Watching the film, they seemed to me to be well intentioned but in a very difficult and fraught way, and their practice must have made for some long and trying nights.

In the mid 1980s, the Atlantis Community left Donegal and relocated to the interior of a Colombian jungle. They are still out there, and they deserve proper notation in the as yet unwritten radical history of the west of Ireland.

————

There was also at large in the 1970s a community of souls said to be shy to the point of muteness—as shy as small birds. They dressed in Victorian clothes. They varied their location between the counties of Mayo, Sligo and Donegal, and they would be seen among the hedgerows, and on the beaches, in white flowing blousons and in breeches, and in high polished boots, in frock coats and stovepipe hats, and they did not speak to the locals ever—not a word—but smiled, ever warmly, when they approached as strangers, and then passed by again, as a scent on the air passes by.

But it was the case increasingly as the decade aged that such esoterica in the Irish west was not uncommon and it quickly got to the point where it could be left unremarked. By the late

1970s, these odd communities had been coming to settle for the best part of a decade. Among the first to arrive, as far as these phenomena can be reliably documented, were the Diggers.

———

Early in 1971, John Lennon summoned Sid Rawle to the offices of Apple Records in London. Rawle was written up in the English press at this time as the "King of the Hippies." He was involved with setting up alternative communities in the rural fringes. He was among the first of a type that would later be characterised as "New Age Travellers." Lennon offered Rawle the custodianship of Dorinish Island. He wanted to find out if a battalion of freaks could thrive cut off from the mainstream and from mainstream values. Rawle accepted the offer and began to spread word around likely London enclaves of an imminent voyage. A group of eighteen adults and a baby was conscripted. The plan was to make a six-week summer camp on the island and evaluate its feasibility as a long-term base for free living.

The Diggers landed on Dorinish Island in June 1971.

———

The window of the room marked nine at the Amethyst Hotel was cracked, and a breeze came through from the May afternoon and sang about the room as a low, eerie, strung-out keening. I sat on the single bed that was in the room, its mattress damp and foul-smelling, and I closed my eyes and listened as closely as I could to what might be heard in such a room, at such a time and in such a place. The world was full of sighs, and the sea moved outside and the wind caught in a shelter break of trees and the sea searched out the crannies of the coast with the tip of its green tongue. The seabirds travelled and called. Outside the room then I heard footsteps but it could not be. I closed my eyes; my heart raced; I heard footfall. It moved as a slow shuffling across the old boards out there, and back again, and forwards again—one-two-three, one-two-three—and I could hear above it all the breath-of-sea—one-two-three, one-two-three—and the footsteps moved, as though two pairs moved in a slow, waltzed rhythm, and it was a May afternoon, again, and time moved hardly at all in the room marked nine at the Amethyst Hotel.

———

The Diggers raised a village of tents. They scoured out hollows in the ground to hold their food. They set vegetable patches and raised stone walls for windbreaks. The soil on Dorinish was good and the patches took easily. Once a fortnight, an oyster boat stopped by and brought a delegation to Westport town to buy groceries there. The group stayed on the island for about a year and a half. Most of the original commune remained intact, and there were others that came and went, but late in 1972, a fire of mysterious origin destroyed the main supplies tent and the Diggers started to move from Dorinish in small groups.

Sid Rawle was the last holdout. For the final days of the Diggers' reign on Dorinish Island he was alone out there. When

I later found a fish-farmer to bring me to the island, he told me a story from his father's time, a story about Rawle being taken from Dorinish. He was cold and starving and close to raving. He was brought to the pub near Murrisk Pier and fed whiskey and sandwiches. He didn't say much that night but later he would say that Dorinish was heaven and it was hell. He returned to Britain and was soon among the founders of the Tipi Valley commune in the Forest of Arden, the first of the major New Age Traveller encampments; almost two hundred people lived there for the best part of twenty years.

I was seeking a contact for Sid Rawle in 2012 when word filtered through that he had died suddenly at a festival outside Leeds at the age of seventy.

———

Whatever it is that you're most scared of surfacing in your work, you can be sure that it's nearby.

I have always been both repelled by and drawn to sentimental forces. I lived in Liverpool for two years and thought it the most sentimental city on earth, with the possible exception of Glasgow. Sentimentality was an enveloping mist that clung to the skin as I walked on a summer night the ale-scented streets; it was there in the timbre of the voices, as the lairy city gulls hovered above, and it was in the watery gleam of the same old man's eyes that seemed to peer from every pub I passed by. It was a city that seemed nostalgic for its own youth and self, and I wallowed in the mawkishness as though to spite myself.

As a ten-year-old, what I seemed to find most distressing about the fact of a recently dead mother was the seeming mawkishness of having to admit to one. Suddenly unmoored, I needed to accomodate the event within the realm of normalcy, and to do so, it needed to be relegated to the back of the mind, to the dark recesses, and as a child you cannot tell what work it will do once planted back there, you cannot predict the ways in which it will pin you down and mark you always, but neither can you predict the ways in which it will set you free.

Now when I think of that event—her name was Josephine—it is usually to see how I might use it and manipulate it to add depth and resonance to my work but without allowing sentimentality to creep pinkly through.

———

What I mean to say is that I wanted to Scream.

The idea was that I would get to the island and I would Scream, I would Scream until I was hoarse and my throat was cut and ribboned, and I would let out all of the green bile that seeps up in a life—the envy, the jealousy, the meanness— and I would let out all of the hate—especially the hate—and I would Scream to the grey sky above me and Scream to the stars and taunt the night.

I intended to spend three days and three nights on Dorinish Island. I imagined this was going to be an odd, meditative interlude in my life—three days of utter inwardness; an exploration of inner space; a seablown breeze to clear all the webs away—and I would return to report my findings in a mature, honed prose, as clear as glass: this from a man who had never knowingly underfed an adjective.

Early on another May afternoon, I cycled the ten miles from Westport to Murrisk Pier. I arrived just as the fish-farmer docked his boat. I do not have the words for boats. I can say only that it was a small boat with an outboard motor. I felt ladylike and impractical as I was helped onto the boat. I carried an Arctic sleeping bag and a small backpack that contained food, notebooks and a bottle of whiskey. I had a mobile phone for use only in emergencies. We set off for Dorinish. I was boyishly excited but also I felt a little sheepish. The boat slapped hard against the waves as it zipped smartly across the water. Small islands came into view as locket shapes and faded as quickly. There was an island shaped like a boot spur; there was an island shaped like a scimitar moon. It was cold on the water and my stomach looped on the dip and rise and the quick sloping of the boat as it moved across Clew Bay. Once a valley I was among its clouds. The tips of its peaks came into view as knuckles and mounds. I recognised Dorinish at once as it appeared: a pair of sisterly cliffs that rise as buttresses against the Atlantic. The engine cut as the boat was worked with tidy skill close to the stones of the island. I climbed out and made it through the foaming ebb of the tide and onto the shore. The fish-farmer waved as he departed again for the length of three days and three nights.

I was alone then on the island.

———

John Lennon published two books of stories or prose fragments: *In His Own Write* and *A Spaniard in the Works*. His
style is built on heavy punning and the formation of madcap compound words that roll out across trippy sentences.
At its very occasional best, it has a playfulness and comic
intelligence that reads something like Spike Milligan as shot
through Dylan Thomas or James Joyce. In fact, he had a
teenage obsession with Thomas that persisted into his adult
years, and later, when his first book appeared and was duti-
fully compared to Joyce, he bought a copy of *Finnegans Wake*,
and he read a few pages and loved it—he said it sounded like
the voice of an old friend—but he couldn't be bothered to
read any more than those few pages.

His own stories, or fragments, suggest great potential but
read like first drafts. His prose writing flitters along the surface of things only, and it is funny and vivid and pacy, but it
never slows or comes down through the gears sufficiently to
allow moments of tenderness, sadness, love, anger, bitterness, or rancour, all the sweet and thorny emotions he rou-
tinely sprang in his brilliant and nerveless songwriting.

———

He wanted to walk out in the world. He began to make odd
excursions. In 1978, he visited Japan alone. He flew there
via South Africa—he carried just a single overnight bag. He
had a couple of hours stopover in South Africa and he asked

a cabdriver to show him some of the country. The driver brought him to a park where he just sat quietly for a while. In Japan, he walked into a hotel and for the first time in his life he booked a room for himself. He walked the streets and nobody could see him. He stepped onto a ferry and stood among the crowd of commuting workers on the deck and kept his eyes down and found to his delight that he was invisible there.

———

The first of the famous photographs are from his teenage teddy boy phase in the late 1950s. "Teddy," of course, abbreviates from Edwardian; the teddy boy fashion of this time was essentially a reprise of the dandyish look adopted by gangs of mostly Irish street boys in Salford and Liverpool in the 1880s. They were at that time known as Scuttlers, and they were very cool and extremely vicious. I came to see him essentially as a kind of Edwardian type: the Melancholy Dandy. It was suggested in the way that he carried himself. And the way that we carry ourselves is dictated primarily, I believe, by the secret airs and reverberations of our places.

———

There is a natural roll or jauntiness to the step when you walk down Bold Street on a busy afternoon. The street is alive with youthful energies; Bold Street is where the cooler kids hang about in their dapper regiments and they have a natural swagger in Liverpool, a kind of haughty belligerence lacked by their contemporaries in London or Dublin. Fashion houses still send scouts to walk the Liverpool streets and report on what the teenage kids are wearing and how they're cutting their hair.

My afternoon routine was to have coffee at the FACT cinema near the top of Bold Street and then shop at Matta's Middle Eastern deli about halfways along. I walked daily the roll of the street, and very often I experienced an overwhelming sense of *déjà vu*, because for all its vibrancy there is an air of otherness or of past times about the street, too. I was not yet aware that Bold Street is the site of more reported paranormal activity than anywhere else in Britain.

———

A time slip occurs on the street. It is usually documented as happening in the vicinity of the old Lyceum post office, by the side entrance to Central station and opposite Waterstones bookstore. A typical report, from 2002, carried in the Liverpool *Daily Post*, came from a former policeman who went shopping on the street with his wife one Saturday afternoon. They emerged from Central station. He met a friend and stopped to talk for a moment. His wife went ahead to Waterstones. When he went to follow, he saw the name "Cripps" above the bookstore, and he jumped back at the honking of a motor horn from an old-fashioned van with the name "Cardin's" on its side. Everywhere on the street the women wore full skirts and had permed hair; the men wore mackintoshes and hats. He crossed the street and the window of the store contained not books but old-fashioned women's shoes, umbrellas, handbags. He felt panicked and he asked a lady beside him, who wore contemporary dress, if this store didn't sell books. Equally bemused, she said that she thought it did, too, and she turned away. He entered the store and there was his wife among the stacked paperbacks, and he looked outside and the street had returned to the moment again.

There have been more than a hundred similiar reports over the years. Almost all of them relate to the area around the Lyceum post office on Bold Street. All the reports suggest that the time slip that occurs leads into the 1950s.

———

I was removed from Dorinish Island in a state of distress. The fish-farmer brought me back to Murrisk Pier and to the same pub that Sid Rawle had been taken to and in much the same condition. Though I had lasted a day and a half as opposed to a year and a half. I had a toasted ham and cheese sandwich and five glasses of red wine. Weak as a kitten, I felt in no condition to cycle back to Westport, and so I phoned a friend there and asked her to drive out and collect me. When she arrived and saw the state that I was in, she actually *shuddered*.

How do I look? I said.

Shook, she said.

Very shook, she said.

What the fuck happened you? she said.

I don't know if I can go into it, I said.

———

By the next morning, however, I felt greatly restored, and I decided to light out for Achill again. I had the sense—perhaps hysterically—that the fibres of the story were starting to knit together. I cycled from Westport to Newport, skirting once more the edges of Clew Bay. Here and there between the trees a view opened up across the water to the knuckle of Croagh Patrick and each time it appeared I raised a knuckle of my own in ritual salute. I hummed little songs as I pedalled along. I stopped for a while in Newport. Anytime I've been through the town I've entered it in sadness and left in something close to happiness—its trapped feeling or reverb, plainly, is a benevolent one.

There was a café tucked away in a corner of the square. I went and sat there for a while. I made some notes about what might be seen from the attic floor of the hotel in the square. A pair of old farmers came into the café and made their order at the counter. They took a table and talked quietly together; they seemed so easy in their skins. They made light work of enormous sandwiches stuffed with ham and coleslaw and lettuce and there were pots of tea and cream cakes to follow. Then one of them looked over at me and rather sternly said—

Wouldn't you enjoy your life?

I left the café and aimed the bike due west for Achill Sound. As I cycled along I heard a train that had not passed this way for years, the rhythm of its heavy clanking along the ruts and ribs of the earth, and I imagined all the faces at the windows, in a blur as they went by, and their tiny sadnesses, and all of them were lost again to the years since they'd passed.

The mountains to the north were hardfounded against grey light.

A thin rain descended on the day in slow drifts and sang.

I came at last on a view of Achill Sound—I got off the bike and stood for a while in the drizzle and watched the white-caps break and each wave as it gave out was the ghost-trace of some lost feeling and a shiver in the blood.

The water moved beneath and slapped against the stakes of the bridge as I cycled across. The streets of the village at Achill Sound were empty as if the world had been about for a while but had moved on again. I took the road by the water and I climbed the mountain by the road and after something less than an hour the road crested and I looked down on the bay at Keel and it was filled darkly as though with blood.

It was the middle of the afternoon when I came to the beach at Keel. I walked it for a long while. I sat on the rocks and was mesmerised by the water. My breath slowed to almost nothing. I saw the women as they crept out of the air in their cloaks of black and waded, and moved out, and screamed their grief to the sky and sea. The shapes of their heavy thighs showed under the wet black of their clothes in the saltwater and the wrack. They screamed and turned finally to face me in their stepped generations and each of them wore my own face—

Lah-de-dah
Lah-de-dum-dum-dah.

———

He believed that the force of a cataclysmic event could smash past a creative block. If such an event placed one in mortal danger and was accompanied by a tremendous crack-up, so much the better.

In the summer of 1980, after heavy weather had sent all of her crew to their bunks with nausea, he was left to sail single-handedly a yacht called the *Megan Jaye* from Rhode Island to Bermuda. He attributed his even and settled stomach to his macrobiotic diet.

The storm grew more ferocious as the night passed and it looked like the end for a while—the Atlantic was grabbing from all sides—and he was panicked and tearful and screamed for God to come take him because he didn't fucking care no more anyhow, and then he lost his mind for a long stretch of sea, and he grew frantic and giddy as the seas raved and the skies opened, and he sang his old songs—he belted them out from his lungs as charms—and he Screamed, and after a long hard night fraught with death-fear and the odd hilarity of disasters he made it at last to calm waters and a placid morning—Bermuda—and he believed that it was this event or passage that cleared his mind and allowed him, after four barren years, to create new material and work again.

———

At the small hotel in Keel, I managed to arrange a room and get through the accompanying small talk without mentioning anything about the unsettling vision on the beach. I was watchful of my tone, however—never in itself a good sign—and I worried that I may have been acting overly cheerful or hearty. The young lady at reception was pleasant and told me about some nearby walking and cycling routes. I said I'd see what the old legs had left to give, and I tried to keep the exclamation marks out of my speech. She said I was in room number nine and smiled quietly as she handed over the key. She asked me did I care to dine at the hotel that evening and I said well, certainly, yes, a reservation for one, please, and now I worried that my diction was becoming too formal, in a kind of weirdly over-comma'd Victorian way. Basically, I was all over the shop, and I was anxious again to the pit of my gut: I decided this meant that the story was starting to come together.

———

I established myself in the room marked nine without significant incident. I smoked a little weed for calm, exhaling out the window so as not to activate the smoke detector. Now what we have here, I said to myself, is such an old, old question: how do you bring up the fact of ghosts in reasonable company? Especially in the reasonable company of one's readers? I was looking out to the hills and the backs of the village buildings as I pondered this—I realised I was actually looking out at the back of the local police station and quickly put my pipe away—and I was feeling much more settled and together in myself, and thinking a little about the story but in a necessarily vague way, just letting it sit at the back of my mind, just there on the ledge of the subconscious where all stories must for a long while sit and season—or so at least I convince myself; no pressure, don't rush it, and so forth— and it occured to me that the 1970s is by now essentially an historical fiction. True memory of the era—as in sense memory, as in the precise tang on the air of a new morning back then, or the throb and rumble of a great city rising from its fumes in the early morning back then, or the way a lover's dark hair might splay just so on the sheets, and she stretches—has by now succumbed to time and distance, and what's left to us is mediated, and it can only be built up again in gimcrack reconstructions, with scenic facade, but if we can get the voices right, the fiction might hold for a while at least.

———

The Liverpool accent, or at least the city accent as it can be heard within, say, a two- or three-mile radius of Lime Street station, is closely related to an Irish accent. There is a type of Liverpool accent that bleeds in particular into the accent of the northside of Dublin. But of course this is an old and storied migration, and one that is stitched into the lore of countless thousands of families: the cities are cousinly.

James and Jane Lennon left County Down in 1848 and emigrated to Liverpool. Among their children was John or Jack Lennon, variously described as a freight clerk or a book-keeper, and also known to be something of a bar-room crooner. Jack married first a Liverpudlian, Margaret Crowley, who died during the birth of their second child. He then married Mary "Polly" Maguire, from Dublin, and they had fifteen children, seven of whom survived. Among these was Alfred, or Freddie, who was John Lennon's father.

Following the death of her husband—the liver—Polly could no longer afford to look after all the children, and Freddie was deposited in the Bluecoat orphanage in 1921. Later, he is variously described as a ship's steward or a merchant seaman, and he was also known to be something of a bar-room crooner.

John became obsessed for a while with these Irish roots. He wrote anti-English songs. He named his second child Sean. He consulted the usual books of heraldry and sources of lineage—slow winter nights at the Dakota—including MacLysaght's *Irish Families: Their Names, Arms and Origins*, in which he learned that the O'Lennons were most typically from the Counties Down, Sligo or Galway, and were not known to have distinguished themselves in military affairs. Late in his life, he spoke of renewing the planning permission for Dorinish Island and building a magical house out there.

Part Seven

SLIP INSIDE THIS HOUSE

Cornelius?

Yes, John?

There's a lot of fucking water.

It's Clew Bay, John.

I mean in the fucking boat.

Oh?

It's up to me ankles.

Okay.

What does this mean, Cornelius?

It means there's a hole in the boat, John.

Alright then.

I wouldn't worry about it. Do you see behind you? There's a basin.

You mean I'm fucking *bailing* now?

It could be a notion.

Cornelius?

John?

I want you to look at my fucking ankles.

Yeah . . . They're soaking alright.

Is fucking right they are!

Do you want me to stop the fucken sea?

Just fucking answer me . . . Are we going to make it to the island?

Touch and go, I'd say. Different question for you.

Yes?

Does it matter, at the end of the day, which island I let you down on?

How'd you mean?

There are hundreds of the fucken things. They are all small, wet, miserable holes of places. They're only fit for hares and rats and filthy birds. Why should one of them be any better or worse than the next?

Listen to me, Cornelius, please. If I was to say to you the words *ritual excursion* . . .

Ho ho.

Ho ho fucking what?

You mean like an aboriginal buck?

In fact that's pretty much exactly what I mean.

The aboriginal is an odd buck.

Are there . . . Are there rats on the islands?

Crawling with them. Night and day. Chorus of them. A squealing fucken choir. But your aboriginal, if I'm not wrong, is the buck who'd be listening?

Exactly so.

What's it he'd be listening for again?

A kind of a song but it's beneath the skin of the earth.

I've heard it.

You've heard which?

The what-you-call-it. The song.

When was this?

I was coming home from a disco in Castlebar.

Okay.

I took a wrong turn.

This was late on?

Thirty-five o'clock in the morning. I found myself moving across a small difficult field. Oh-oh, I says. Where this field was exactly you could nail me to the cross and crucify me and I'd still not be able to tell you. But I found that an awful shiver had come into me. It was as if the blood had turned to ice in my veins. The feeling was not of this world but of another.

Cornelius?

Stay with me. I turned around. I was sure there was someone behind me. There was nothing and there was nobody. I thought there'd be eyes in the dark. There were no eyes, John. But the dark seemed to close in around me. As if it was trying to take hold of me. I was moved slowly around on my innocent feet. It was like I was being turned on my feet by a dancing partner.

Was it the devil?

Ah go easy, John, would you? I felt like I was being lifted above the ground.

Was it a floating sensation?

Well. I was . . . aloft. Is the only way I could say it for you.

Okay.

Aloft!

And what happened next?

All the air got sucked out of the world. There was utter quiet. And I could see everything. Do you know that kind of way? I could see the smallest things and the biggest. I could see across the sea and I could see over the shoulders of the mountains and I could see down a maggot's ears.

There were maggots?

Next thing there was . . . Jesus Christ . . . I don't know . . . I could only call it a rip in the sky.

Okay.

I'm not joking you. A rip! And I looked into it. And what did I see?

This I want to hear.

I saw the bottom of the fucken sea. And it was deserted except for all the little floaty plants and the rocks and the one . . . small . . . wise-lookin' . . . crab.

A crab?

Is right.

And wise?

And tuneful, John. Because it fucken sang to me.

Cornelius?

Don't ask me the words. Stretch me out on the Spanish rack and I could not repeat for you the words. But I could tell you the feeling it gave me handy enough.

Go on then.

Utter peace, John. Cornelius O'Grady wasn't made of bones and flesh and woes no more. All I was made of was a pure fucken smile and glee.

You were floating still?

Across the night and sky and not a bother on me. Well, I says to myself, this is a good one.

How'd it wind up, Cornelius? For a finish?

I came to, John.

I'd imagine so.

On the flat of my back in the middle of the same field and it pissing out of the heavens on me.

Morning?

And as bleak as you'd meet one. You know you've a night of it put down when you wake up in a small wet field.

There seems to be an amount of that around here.

Why would you think that is?

I don't know.

Because the fields are possessed, John.

You say this matter-of-factly, Cornelius.

Well.

———

Cornelius cuts the motor—the boat coasts by the sea road. There are voices in the night. There is a car on the stones of a small beach. There are men talking in a pod of smoke and carlight. They are very close but the boat moves unseen and silently by stealth through the water.

Pressmen, Cornelius says.

A voice comes clearly for a moment as they pass—

If she goes on me again it'll be the last time she goes. Thirty pound that exhaust.

Steepish, Cornelius says.

The world's about, John says.

———

Home bites at him for a bit. But he will not go back there. The days of England are done for now. What the fuck is England good for? Sausages and beer and pale gawpy faces. He sits in the boat and he fucking well bails. On white porcelain cups in railway cafés the lipstick traces. The boat moves on its slow-boom beat and it dips and scoops and cuts through the water. His gut is all over the shop. His heart aches for old England. The dark sky growls; in the near low mountains there are rumbles.

Mother of fuck, Cornelius says.

I've made a misery of your father's suit, John says, bailing.

It's not much good to him where he is now.

Do you ever think about where that might be?

I do, actually.

I thought you might.

I would see it as a falling field that runs down to the sea, John. It is not a bad old day there at all. Maybe it's much the same as now, the Maytime. From the field you can look across the sea or at least across a wide clean pacified bay. It's calm as glass. You walk in this field but of course by your nature you make no shade. The sun is through the white clouds in the sky but there is not much heat in it. By the edge of the field, by the shadow of the ditch, it feels very cold. You walk but your step doesn't land. You are at an elevation in the air just a fraction above the thistles and the heads of the flowers. You are no more than a few inches in the air but it puts a lovely ease into the motion. You are stepping through the air. Your eyes are speckled in the way that a young fox's are, greenishly. There is a particular type of saltiness on the air and it's of the sex. Your whole body from head to toe is weightless and trembles with delight. The breeze off the bay is a light one but plenty all the same to move you around the place. You travel the field hither and back again. Everything is very funny. The way a sheep looks up at the sky. The way the wren darts from a hole in the stone wall on its happy bouncing rear. The fucken hilarity of it all. The world has no sorrows. The world is nothing but a long comfortable sighing. The field runs down to the sea. The blood still pulses as in the best days of rude fucken youth. Certainly, John, it is in the west of Ireland.

———

They move out across the bay. The weather turns. With each moment the bay becomes rougher. There are sentimental forces at work. Also there is deathhauntedness—it is written across the sky. Cornelius steers with a blithe hand to the tiller. His eyes are vague and cheerful. The sky is moving above us now and ever so darkly. John is losing track of himself again. Which may be the purpose. Trouble is a cloak that I choose to wear. The boat moves; the past is about. Old England has him again, as it always will—he's a Second War kid. He screamed to life in the tinpot metropolis and a thousand nazi bombs came down to mark the occasion. There was sexy Adolf in his dancing boots. There were death planes on the English skies. Now the gulls wheel in sudden calm above Clew Bay and the bay pacifies but just for a beat and there is a sharp, hard slap of water and everything giddies and turns again and he thinks: what's the worst that can happen us out here? Plenty the fucking worst.

Cornelius?

Yes, John?

What I'm thinking now is fuck it, you know, the first island we come to?

I'm thinking the same way.

With these words it sails into view. It is not his island but another. The boat tilts deftly for it. The boat scalps froth from the water. The small island sits waiting in the wind and wild rain; it sits infinitely in grey patience. This island has at once a maudlin or a mawkish air. He has not put his foot to its stones and he's come over solemn and searching again—

After a while, Cornelius, do you get to wondering?

About, John?

What's it we're here for?

You mean in the middle of Clew Bay on as miserable a fucken Sunday as you'd meet?

Or more generally.

Ah Jesus, John. Are you having feelings again?

I know.

These large sad warmish feelings, John? The best thing you can do is ignore the fucken things.

I wish that I could. I wish I could think of nothing but the happy things. The kid and love and home and all the rest of it. I wish I could think about the fucking money. But then I get thrown back in again. I'm into the past and the murky things. I am not in control, Cornelius, of the way my fucking brain turns. You know where I'm at sometimes? Just by way of hysterical fucking example? I'm in nineteen twenty fucking dot. I'm in the Bluecoat orphanage. How fucking cruel and how fucking lonely? To lie awake at night in the middle of the city. No brothers here, no sisters. A kid awake in the city and lonely. It's the winter and deep in. This gimpy fucking kid in the corner bed. This snotfaced raggedy limpy kid. The best part of you's dripped down your dad's leg, hasn't it, Freddie?

Ah, John.

And I will not wipe these tears away. My old man? He was like me without the spark plug in. I could have been a fucking disaster as easy. It's like aunt always said—I'm just the idiot that got lucky.

Can you not go easy on yourself the one time, John?

No I fucking cannot.

———

The island is as drab as its first glance suggested. They push through the misery of its weather across the stones of a shingle beach. The wind is that stiff it raises the eyebrows. Weather that outrages. The stones slide and click eerily beneath their feet as they go. The click and fall of the old Chinamen's dominoes, on Berry Street, in the Liverpool afternoons—it's the same note and bone sound precisely. Throwing the bones they called it in the Liverpool pubs.

Cornelius as he ploughs into the weather is happiness itself, is native to the murk, rain and shifting wind.

Above us, John, are you watching?

His words come cupped in a pocket of the wind. The remnants of a cottage sit on a rise above the shoreline. It is huddled sourly among the rocks there. They climb to it. The half-crumbled walls stand about like bewildered soldiers. He steps inside the roofless hollow; Cornelius steps in after. They lean back against the walls of the place. The walls and the men hold each other up. Throwing the bones—doesn't it mean also to read the future? They are out of the wind here at least. They consider each other coolly.

What was your plan, John?

Fuck off, Cornelius.

———

The way the sky is squared off by the half-fallen walls. Nothing between them and the heavens now. Snipes of wind get through the gaps with fast enquiries but they're away again as quick. The wind about the bay and the rain make arbitrary music. I wanted to be stood out in the world and here I fucking well am. Here I am on this commanded journey. The sky moves and it is dark and light at once. Size of the place? You'd hardly have kept a family here. Though people were smaller, a world of full-growns five foot two, the kids like elves. The stones that are blackened still must be the last of the fireplace. He lights a fag. So the fireplace was just there, and maybe the huddled sleepers there—a family—and were their limbs entwined, for warmth and love, against the wind and island night?

No, John. This place would have had no more than a poor farmer in it. And only for a few weeks at a time, for the sheep, in summer.

I see.

Hauling the maggot out of his stomach and drinking green envy and spitting into the fireplace.

You paint it beautifully.

My own father used these places, John. He would cross over in the springtime and the summer. We would not see him for weeks on end. Which was a relief to all fucken parties. He was not right in himself ever nor right in the world. There were times he was so bad he couldn't lift a cup of tea to his face. Do you want tea, my mother would say, or more likely she would ask me to say. The father would look back at me, with the eyes like stones inside his head, and he'd say, I no more want tea, Cor, and he would look away and settle down lowly to himself. Like a wounded animal settling to its lair. There was no easy relief for him. The way that he groans—I can hear it still, John, I can hear the same groans exactly rise up from myself some mornings. It's then I fucken worry. Did you know that the groans get passed down to us? My father would bring sheep out to the islands in the summer. I wonder if he was easier in himself when he was on his own. I'd doubt it. He was an intelligent man but it would lead him—the same mind—into dark and difficult places. He would travel inside himself. He would go utterly quiet. You'd know that he was gone deep and to someplace bad because all the colour would leave his face. As if someone turned the bar off on an electric fire—as quick as that. He would go very pale and I would say nothing and my mother would say nothing and I would go outside but I wouldn't even kick a ball against the gable. It might take an hour or two for it to pass, sometimes a week. He would move lightly through the yard then and you would know it had passed because he would say right so, Cor, and he might even rub my head. The colour would not yet be back in his face. Wherever it was that he had been. But he would move with a bit of a skip to him to reassure me and to make out he was the finest again.

And now it's Cornelius weeping.

Fathers and sons, isn't it?

Oh fuck off, John! You have me fucken ragged.

———

They wait out the weather against the walls of the memorious ruin. He looks through the fallen window and onto the bay. A white Spanish horse races across the low waves. This is news he should keep to himself. He squints his eyes halfways shut to make it a trick of the light—the horse stops and turns and raises onto its hind legs and snorts pale fire. It takes off again into the mist and distance. John falls into a huddle and grips himself hard and shuts his eyes to break the spell.

What's the latest, John?

As a matter of fact, Cornelius, I think I've come loose of my fucking bean completely.

No wonder. The wind is after shifting east. There's none of us right when the wind shifts east.

But I'm having vision-type fucking things, Cornelius!

It would surprise me if you weren't.

———

The weather continues as roughly.

He has a fag and listens hard.

He travels.

I'm away again, he says.

Where've you landed, John?

On fucking Mount Street. I'm thinking of the late fifties. It's a night in the winter and there's a vicious wind come up the town. At this time I'm at the art college. My head's all over the road. It's early in the nighttime and I'm stood outside the art college. I'm stood at the corner of Mount Street and Pilgrim Street. I'm talking to some goon about his new band he's got up and he's asking about band names and what do you think of this, John, and what do you think of that, John, and I've no idea what it is he's gone and called his fucking band, The Flying Testicles, what-fucking-ever, and I'm going yeah, alright, that's good is that, and it's then his face starts to give.

Give?

I don't know how to describe this, Cornelius. But the years are peeling off and time is shifting.

I know the way.

He becomes a different person. He comes from some other time. He is away out of this cold winter, he says, and this miserable air and he tells me about Spanish places and the port of Càdiz and the orange trees in fucking Màlaga, all this, and he'll miss his girl so much—her long brown hair—and he'll miss his dotey Irish mam—and I cannot get away quick enough I'm that spooked. I walk off and wave and he goes, so long then, John, and I'm away up Rice Street, I'm away for Ye Cracke—it's early in the night and empty—and I sit in the war room on my own, a pint of bitter, in the snug, and I have a fag, try to settle, and the city is moving outside me, all around me, like it's come loose, and I don't know where the fuck I am nor when and you know what I'm saying to myself?

What?

I'm saying—

Cling the fuck on, John.

———

Cornelius?

Yes, John?

Do you think about your old man still?

It wouldn't be a happy dream for me, John. Did I not say? He topped himself for a finish.

Oh. I'm sorry.

He was nearly as well off out of it. And what good would it do to think of him in that place he went to?

No good. You must not ever think of that place. You must not ever think of that dark and glamorous place.

———

How did it happen, Cornelius?

Well. In the same way that an old dog gets to a certain age and a level of disregard for itself and it just takes off some night into the bushes. My father heard what was coming for him. And we didn't find him after, in the way you wouldn't find an old dog—you just wouldn't—because my father, I have no doubt, put himself in the sea. It was all his life nearby and it would have been an idea always of a way out. He would not have been the type to string himself from the rafter of a barn. He was considerate. There was no show in the man.

———

Evening moves across the bay. With it there comes a calmness that could be taken almost for reason. The wind drops to near enough nothing. They leave the sour ruin gladly and make for the boat again. It puts out to the dark water.

We're getting closer, John. Despite ourselves.

The boat moves across the bay. The tiny islands rest and idle in the evening light. His heart comes down to a slow, dull, even thumping. In no time at all the cliffs of Dorinish Island can be made out in a clear aspect, rising.

Oh there, he says.

They come at last to his island.

There's a tube of toothpaste in the suitcase, John. There's a brush to go with it. There is a small bottle of whiskey for emergency situations. There are tins of beans and matches and there are kindling sticks dried well. There will be rain in spats but this place will dry you as quick as it'll wet you. There's bread. There is a package of cooked ham cut thick in slices. Ate the fucken ham whatever you do. If you come across on the rocks a large greenish egg not much smaller than the size of your own head and speckled, I want you to walk a long, slow curve around it—it'll be a tern's egg and the fucken mother will have your eyes out if you go near it and it would be an awful thing for a man to lose an eye to a maddened bird on his own small island in Clew Bay. Do you hear me, John?

Yes, Cornelius, I'm listening.

———

He stands on the island and waves as the boat moves slowly back to its own world. He has the belted leather suitcase by his feet. He wears the old man's suit. The gulls hover above the water to reel down the night. The first lights are beading across the mainland now. He listens intently—oh let there be a sign that this is not the end place. The hollow sound the sea makes speaks of nothing so much as the hushed quiet of the big sleep that's to come, maybe soon, maybe late. The island is cold and loud with birds—he is too scared to turn and face into it. The boat becomes smaller in the distance; it disappears. He tries to put himself together again. His lips move to make words and he looks out for a long time over the dark water. He is falling again. He wants to be home now and away from this cold place. He wants never to feel this old again. The mainland lights are many and hopeful across the distance of the water.

———

He turns in to face the island at last. It is so very fucking cold out here on the rocks. The stones talk beneath his feet as he moves along the shifting, clicking causeway and the night birds huddle and thrum in the crevices and gaps and make their slow contented hums—it's in the dim haze of the night that he can see clearly at last. The lights on the mainland are arranged as a song and in quite an eerie notation, actually—he hums it for a bit and all the birds quieten. He is terrified and ecstatic and he goes from the east to the west of himself. Small voices come off the water. The water moves and there is a boat in the dark—again they have come for him. There are men huddled on the boat as her engine cuts and the boat lights up with torches and shows the men, with their fags and flasks, and he does not fucking fear them and he stands tall on a high rock to look out and face them and the boat comes ever the closer and one of the men rises in the torchlight and calls—

Mr. Lennon? Would you like to make a statement?

Abso-fucking-lutely, he says.

———

Have you got your paper and pens handy? Are you ready to press "record"? Then, gentlemen, I shall begin. I am made of rags and bones and tattered skin. I am of the third sex. My spirit animal is the billy goat or perhaps some days it's the hare. I'm never quite sure, in fact. I come and go in time and fucking space. Hobbies? I quite like to speak on the telephone. I do like a good yap. I talk to Liverpool, I talk to Hy-Brasil, I talk to fucking Mars. I like to put my voice along the high wires. I could quote you some poetry if you'd like?

How're you fixed for some Gerard Manley Hopkins? I caught this morning morning's fucking minion—the one where he sees a bird and goes all swoony coz he loves fucking nature. Nature? I've had my fill of it, gents. Turns out it's all an illusion. Pull the fucking drapes back and it'll disappear. It's painted fucking scenery. It's a diorama. I am full of venom and bile and honky fucking blood. I'm afraid you've got me at quite a busy moment. I'm about to crawl under a rock and have a yap with the maggots. Also I'm having quite a difficult time with these terns. They do go on a bit, don't they? If you really must take my photograph, young man, make me beautiful and get my good side. It's this one, actually. This side I look like a young Rita Hayworth. The other side I look like Quasi-fucking-modo. I've always envied a gentleman with a hump. No one's going to ask you why the long face, are they? Now what else can I tell you? The number nine's for Dingle—you won't catch me out on the Liverpool buses. I had a small growth on my back the other month, I thought it was me hump getting started. Turned out to be a boil, which was a disappointment. What else can I tell you? I think we should all love and ravish each other but I'm holding out no great hopes. I might grow into this suit yet, I fully accept it's not a perfect fit. Do go easy on yourselves, gentlemen, you'll not be going around for long. Do have a go at the fat lying hypocrite bastards that run the fucking place, won't you? Smell the flowers and so forth and fuck each other gladly. Any follow-ups, gents? Any further enquiries? A little more Manley Hopkins? Certainly. Blue-bleak embers shall fall, gall themselves and gash gold-vermillion. He was a fucking laugh, wasn't he? Good night, gentlemen. Safe home the sea road.

Part Eight

THE GREAT LOST
BEATLEBONE TAPE

The sound engineer, Charlie Haimes, pushes open the steel door and steps outside to the first of the morning. He sits on the same step of the fire escape that he's sat on almost every morning of these last humid weeks. It is a little after six and already very warm. The bars of the escape are warm to the touch even. He lights another fag, Charlie Haimes. It's late July, and the smoke is a hard burn on his lungs.

Inside a fuzzbox oodles and wafts. An effects unit hisses and barfs. A theremin runs slow eerie loops. A shriek sustains on the long pedal. It all sounds to Charlie Haimes like a cat having an incident. But who is Charlie Haimes to say?

The music dies and there are bootsteps and the steel door opens again—John steps out. He has a face on. He rests on the rail and looks out across the city or what can be seen of the city from the fire escape—the workings of a laundry, the back of a Turkish restaurant, a sliver of the early-morning street. He takes his glasses off and rubs his weary eyes.

JOHN   Heroin, Charlie.

CHARLIE   At the very least, John.

JOHN   Speedballs, Charlie.

CHARLIE   We do need something.

JOHN   A crate of vodka. It sounds fucking cracked in there.

CHARLIE   It does a bit.

JOHN   It sounds like a fucking nuthouse. And not in a good way.

CHARLIE   It's going to be a challenging piece of work.

JOHN   They're going to do me up like a fucking kipper, Charlie.

CHARLIE   Well there are no songs. As such. I mean song-type songs. Is the thing of it, John.

JOHN   You think this is news to me, Mr. Haimes?

CHARLIE   I'm not saying it necessarily needs song-type songs. As such.

JOHN   There are nine fucking pieces.

CHARLIE   But do they flow? As such?

JOHN   Flow, Charlie? What do you think this is? Fucking Supertramp? We're breaking the line.

CHARLIE   We're certainly doing that.

The morning lifts across the city. The first scratches of life are on the air; the first of a summer Thursday's railyard aches and rousing groans.

CHARLIE   The thing about the fuzzbox, John?

JOHN   The thing about the fuzzbox, Charlie, is I don't know how to operate the fucking fuzzbox.

The throb of the first trains from deep as the sun comes slowly higher. It's going to be a blinder. John beads his eyes and sucks on his fag and turns a significant look on the sound engineer Charlie Haimes.

JOHN   "Family Of Three" is getting there. The business with the theremin aside. A single, maybe?

If it had a bloody chorus, thinks Charlie Haimes.

JOHN   It's been a long six weeks, Charlie. But another two and we're done. Or possibly three.

CHARLIE   Which would make it nine for a finish. Incidentally.

JOHN   Yeah, well, the thing about the nines, Charlie, is I'm blue in the face from the fucking nines. I've been seeing the fucking nines everywhere. I've been reading the nines into situations. I've had it up to here with the fucking nines.

They are running on fags and cold tea. John exhales slowly to the morning. Now he turns and considers with fresh interest the sound engineer Haimes.

JOHN   Where is it you're from, Charlie? Originally.

CHARLIE   Douglas way.

JOHN   You mean Isle of bloody Man Douglas?

CHARLIE   Same as.

JOHN   A Manx?

CHARLIE   Brine for blood.

JOHN   Do you think it's coming through, Charlie?

CHARLIE   The which?

JOHN   The point of it all.

CHARLIE   Well . . .

JOHN   Okay.

The air is warmer by the moment. The city's ripe odour is rising. It's like Delhi on a bad day, thinks Charlie Haimes, whose gut has not been right. He's done time in Delhi has Charlie. The charas hashish. Never again with the squidgy black—never again with the charas hashish. One night he'd thought there was a bird talking to him. Another time a chair.

CHARLIE   What does her nibs think?

JOHN   Well her nibs is off the fucking record, isn't she?

CHARLIE   How is that situation by the way? Thaw?

JOHN   Thaw is a strong word, Charlie.

John looks up to the sky and considers the plain white and blue of it—as if there might be answers written up there.

JOHN   What it's about? Fucking ultimately? It's about what you've got to put yourself through to make anything worthwhile. It's about going to the dark places and using what you find there.

John flicks his half-smoked fag. He leans his arms on the bars and his chin on his skinny arms.

JOHN   Here's an odd question, Charlie. Is it, in effect, some kind of occult fucking jazz thing?

CHARLIE   That's definitely a way of looking at it, John.

Morning climbs the white-blue sky. The sound engineer Charlie Haimes wishes that he was at home, in the farmhouse, with Dora, and the nippers, having a spliff and thinking about getting his tomatoes in. *There isn't much Charlie Haimes needs telling about tomatoes.*

CHARLIE   At least we've binned the Irishy bits.

JOHN   There is that. That fucking fiddler?

They have a laugh about the fiddler again. This cuts the tension. The fiddler was five foot nothing and smelt of whiskey and had the eyes of a haggard masturbator. John reckoned he'd been sneaking in the loo to have one off the handle.

JOHN   Used to play with Van Morrison, apparently.

John, hawk-faced, spluttering, one traumatised 4 a.m., had said: Right then! We're done with the fucking fiddles! And I mean in-fucking-toto, Charlie!

JOHN   Maybe I'm not whacked out enough anymore, Charlie. Maybe I'm not as far out my own self as the fucking record is supposed to be.

There isn't a great deal Charlie Haimes can say to that. The sun comes through the backs of the buildings across the way. John's skin is night-work pale in the morning light.

JOHN   What I heard in that cave, Charlie?

CHARLIE   Oh yeah?

JOHN   I'm not even going to say how good it could have been.

John reaches over the rail now and he looks down below. He sighs in long suffering. He slides to a sitting position.

JOHN   I do think that's where they're at, you know? The dead ones. I think they get together out on the water. Else how can you explain all the lonely mopers stood about on the shore?

This is heading into odd country is the view of Charlie Haimes. Though there was the time in Llandudno he'd had a weep about his nan.

CHARLIE   I had a weep about me dead nan in Llandudno one time. On the promenade.

JOHN   Oh?

CHARLIE   I think it was a Sunday. I found myself stood on the prom and bawling out the tears.

JOHN   You were close to your old nan, Charlie?

CHARLIE   That's the odd thing about it, John. I never liked the old witch. She was the tightest woman in Douglas. Which is saying bloody something. She gave me four sausage rolls when I done my Holy Communion.

JOHN   Moony types get drawn to bodies of water, Charlie. They always have done.

CHARLIE   Is what it is.

JOHN   If you wanted me to be fucking French about it?

CHARLIE   Go on.

JOHN   It's because when you look out to sea, you're looking at a fucking infinitude.

CHARLIE   Of?

John joins his hands to make a seashell—a conch?—and blows inside and opens his hands again—puff—as though to free a dove.

JOHN   An infinitude, Charlie, of nothingness.

CHARLIE   Heroin, John.

JOHN   At the very fucking least, Charlie.

CHARLIE   You want to go back in?

He doesn't answer. The silence that holds is easier now and London is pinkly waking. They've been through a lot together. The rattling of the bones; the squalls and the screeching; the occult shimmers; the lonely airs; the sudden madcap waltzes; the hollowed voices; the sibilant hiss; the asylum screams; the wretched moans; the violence, love, and tenderness—beatlebone. The first of the buses goes past at a sprightly chug.

JOHN   Have you ever Screamed, Charlie?

CHARLIE   I have a bit. So happens. In my day.

JOHN   And what did you find, Charlie? When you went inside?

CHARLIE   Not a whole lot to write home about, John. As it turns out.

Charlie Haimes could be enjoying the slow life. He could be tending his veggies and having his puff. But the call came in. Have you anything in the book, Charlie? Not till Kate Bush in October. Well, John's in town. John? John. Do you mean John-John? The same.

JOHN   Are we going to make a record then?

CHARLIE   I daresay we're going to make something.

John pockets his fags; Charlie watches closely.

JOHN   Do you ever think about being a kid, Charlie?

CHARLIE   Sometimes. You see things in your own and it makes you think back.

JOHN   When were you happiest in your life?

CHARLIE   Probably right now.

JOHN   You mean this minute? That's very kind, Charles.

CHARLIE   I mean where I am right now.

JOHN   Wales, isn't it?

CHARLIE   That's right.

JOHN   Doesn't Roger Daltrey keep a trout farm there?

CHARLIE   I believe he does.

JOHN   I tried the countryside. I went off my fucking bean. I tried the city. I can take it or fucking leave it.

CHARLIE   What about this island then?

JOHN   Turns out the thought of it's the thing, Charlie. The reality is slippery rocks and freezing fucking sea and creamy fucking gull shit. Not to mention the banshee fucking wind.

A summer day gets up and about itself. It's going to be a meat-spoiler. It's going to be pig heat in this old, old habitation. He's got the faraway look on. He—John—has gone off to the vaults of darkness again. As if all of it can make no difference, as if each time he opens his mouth it's just a scream to pierce the moment against the darkness that's coming, the void.

CHARLIE   QPR are a lovely young side. They could go well this year. Is my feeling. A very capable young side. Do you follow the football, John?

JOHN   I went to art college, Charlie.

The sound engineer has been around a share of these type blokes in his day. What it is, if you ask Charlie Haimes, is a case of arrested development.

JOHN   You never get past what happens to you when you're seventeen.

Charlie Haimes tries to remember when he was seventeen. 1961? Not bloody yesterday. He was possibly already in Brum by then. Which wasn't without its excitements for a Charlie Haimes, seventeen, fresh fish out of Dudley.

JOHN I'd be coming down Bold Street. Is the feeling that I get. And I was that fucking sharp, Charlie, you know?

The morning is tight as a drum now. The first of the traffic sends out its snarls. The air becomes heavier and tastes of oil and poppers.

CHARLIE There's always the possibility you're breaking new ground here, John.

This goes down very well.

JOHN As in maybe this thing is ahead of its fucking time?

CHARLIE Careful, but.

JOHN It's a very pretty thought.

John stands up and stretches. He groans from his years—he groans from deep inside.

JOHN I'm getting old, Charlie. And I think I might be getting a bit fat again.

There's no odds in engaging here, thinks Charlie Haimes.

CHARLIE Italian caff won't be long opening. We could get a couple of sausage sarnies in?

JOHN   Ooh . . .

John looks wearily now towards the studio door. The drear fucking repetition of it all. It's never a picnic, this.

JOHN   Maybe a trout farm in Wales is the way to fucking go.

CHARLIE   They get lice, trout.

JOHN   Which is neither here nor there, Charlie.

In the studio a tape spools and resets and comes to life again—a sudden squall, a half-rhythm.

JOHN   The fuck?

CHARLIE   I dunno how that's come on.

John stands up to listen; Charlie sits and listens. It's got a low slithering thread, a half-rhythm with a chanted beat, an arcane air.

JOHN   Charlie?

CHARLIE   I know.

JOHN   You hearing this?

CHARLIE   I think I fucking am.

And now the beaten hollows of a chest, and a theremin's loops, and the squall of a fuzzbox, and there are white horses riding the sea. John fishes out his box of fags and he pops one with a squeeze of the box and he lights it. A peregrine falcon crosses the sky.

JOHN   Here's a question for you.

CHARLIE   Okay?

JOHN   In some of this stuff we've put down, right? Is there a weird kind of sex heat coming off?

CHARLIE   A sex heat?

JOHN   A kind of sex feeling. A kind of . . . clammy feeling?

CHARLIE   Can't say as I've noticed, John.

Ever the diplomat, Charlie Haimes, who's been six weeks in the studio trying to look the other way.

JOHN   But fuck it, you know? All that matters is that it's a fucking masterpiece and that it's better than what the rest of the whey-faced cunts are coming up with.

Kate Bush is going to be a walk in the park, thinks Charlie Haimes. And he—John—leans out across the rail and looks to the new morning across the bone-dry city; London hasn't had a drop for weeks.

CHARLIE   I wonder if we shouldn't knock off for now? Come in fresh tonight.

JOHN   Nonsense, Charlie. We'll push on through.

They both stand and turn to look at the steel door that leads to the studio.

JOHN Care less. That's the way to go with this thing, Charlie. Don't you think?

CHARLIE Now you're talking.

JOHN I mean have you heard what Scott Walker's been up to? With his plinkety fucking plonk plonk?

CHARLIE Avant-garde, John. Is what it is.

JOHN My peasant arse. This is going to make Scott Walker sound like the Mamas and the fucking Papas.

I quite liked the Mamas and the Papas, thinks Charlie Haimes. Those were very lovely, those harmonies. Between the backs of the buildings—the laundry, the Turkish restaurant—there's a sliver of street to be seen, and it's Tottenham Street, coming around from Goodge Street station, and here's the old Italian prowling by, always first about the street. He must be tipping eighty, an old-stager, and he'll have the café open any minute now. Charlie's stomach rumbles. He could use a bacon sandwich and a mug of scald.

CHARLIE We could line our stomachs, John?

JOHN I'm good for now. But you look after yourself. I've eaten a pig and a half this last six weeks.

They stay on the fire escape. It must be going on for half past six if the old Italian's about. The heat is building.

JOHN There are times I wish I was a geography teacher in fucking Woolton.

CHARLIE Patches on your elbows and a broken mug for your pipe cleaners.

JOHN Saturdays? I'll nip out for an hour. Teatime. Two and a half pints and a read of the pink. Some peace from the kiddies.

Charlie Haimes hears a stack of newspapers slapped down on Tottenham Street. A shutter rises with a jaunty screech. There is a maniacal holler, indecipherable, from the vicinity of Goodge Street station.

JOHN It's going to be a stinker, Charlie.

CHARLIE It's going to be a tar-melter. You want to go in?

JOHN Let's give it half a tick.

They've been in since nine the evening before. It's going to be another twelve-hour run with a squall of broken notes to show for it. A tubby kid goes by on Tottenham Street with his bucket of paste and the last of his posters. He'll have been plastering the town half the night. Elvis Costello. The Slits. African Head Charge in the Hackney Empire.

JOHN   You notice the way it's the last hour we often get something?

Ever the optimist, thinks Charlie Haimes, who's been having his tinnitus again—a worry—and that's not to mention the bloody piles. A tub of salt, apparently, tipped into a lukewarm bath. Is the way to go for piles. Charlie Haimes has a farmhouse to pay off. The plan is to pack all this in and stick to the homestead on a three-six-five basis. Run the place as a donkey sanctuary. He has a thing for a donkey has Charlie Haimes. There's something about them that's spiritual, kind of. And Dora had two as a kid— Billy Joe and Dixie.

JOHN   I'm going to do some words, Charlie. Just roll a tape and I'll do some words for this fucking thing.

The story has been coming through in odd scraps all summer. He talks about the island and he talks about the cave. Some bloke with one ear—a badger had his other. Charlie Haimes has mixed feelings about badgers. Tuberculosis. Spread of. Or so they say.

John sings a bit in American—an old jingle-type snatch:

JOHN   "Everyday's an holidaaay, at the A-me-thyst 'otel . . ."

Amethyst? Like a jewel? Like a gem? Colour of a bird's eye in the rain? He slaps his hands together, John. He pouts a kiss for the sound engineer Charlie Haimes. He pushes through the steel door.

JOHN   In your own time, Charlie.

CHARLIE   I'll be with you.

JOHN   He's gonna make a hames of it!

CHARLIE   Tell me one I've not heard.

JOHN   He's a proper Charlie!

The morning sun tips over a rooftop. The sea? In fact he was never gone on the sea was Charlie Haimes. Give him a nice placid lake any day.

John sticks his head out again.

JOHN   The way I'm thinking, Charlie, is I'm going to utterly fucking transmute myself.

CHARLIE   Careful how you go.

Charlie counts the fags in his box. Nine. He'll have to nip out for fresh. Cornershop's open for seven. Can show his face in the Italian caff, too. The old-stager will be at his rituals. Wipe the coffee spout, leave out the grease traps. Get your wireless on. Hasten slowly. You make the moments of a day and a life is what you do.

This story that's been coming through? The room marked nine. The crows like Gestapo. The voices in the trees.

JOHN   I'm going to turn myself inside out. I'm going to fucking express myself, Charlie. I'll do the fucking words for this thing. About what happened to me on the island.

CHARLIE   I'll roll a tape, John.

JOHN   Finish your fag first.

CHARLIE   Alright then.

JOHN   And do not lose this fucking tape, Charlie.

He pushes the door out and Charlie Haimes is left to himself for a last few morning moments. It is the Thursday of the week, with a Thursdayish air. Not unhopeful, actually. The emptiness of the street is framed by the shunting of the trains for Goodge Street station. Now a post van slides past and beyond the steel door John is singing—he's lah-lah-lahing—and Charlie stubs his fag on the rail of the fire escape, and inside John is singing—he's hah-hah-hahing—and the coil of the morning tightens and turns.

The sound engineer, Charlie Haimes, rights himself for the last of the work, a new tape to loop and the last tracks to separate, and John is singing inside—he's tra-lah-lahing—and now two kids appear on Tottenham Street, a boy and a girl, and he is long and thin with a mess of hair and she is tiny and they just idle there, and they're looking this way—aren't they?—with a slouched and watchful air, and inside John is singing, and the boy leans into the girl and he speaks to her, and she agrees and they move on again, and there is something about them that unsettles the sound engineer Haimes because about the boy there is something wolfish and about the girl there is the sense of an elf.

———

Charlie Haimes enters the studio and kicks the steel door shut behind. Bolts it. He spools a tape on the Telefunken M12

Magnetophon—tape tension is constant, no need for brake solenoids—and John sits crouched and smoking with a blanket around his shoulders and Charlie rolls the tape, and John begins—

———

[transcript]

and if i have nothing left to say—well okay—because when i have nothing left to say—[indecipherable]—there was an enormous fucking egg on the rocks—is it rolling charlie?—i can see it very clearly in fact—brownish actually with yellow speckles on—do i sound like i'm going to fucking sing, charlie?—i'm on my island at last—an enormous fucking egg the size of me head and bigger again an egg that big a baby baboon might step out pinkarsed—smeared light and blue void—[indecipherable]—i will keep my distance from that fucking egg—it seems to move just a bit—something's got to crack and something's got to give—i'm not having in with that fucking egg—say a newborn john steps out and spits the mucusy bits away—pale and moonfaced—skinny new john with an heron's legs and a reedy chest—a hairless reedy art college chest—poetical—tubercular—it grows worse by the hour, my love—i'll give it some richard fucking burton shall i?—boskier—what's fucking bosky when it's at home?—my words are fucked and all over—in the city my head feels big as a melon—too much noise—on the island my head feels tiny as a pea—i could belly across the rocks and tip my ear up against that giant egg—news therein I daresay—shells and walls and caves and holes and rooms

and hollows—here's a word—encasement—not one to lin-
ger on, doctor—close my eyes—i could walk the rocks for a
while it would kill a fucking hour like a tall dark bird as the
last of the daylight goes on an ink-black stick-bone night-
dark heron's walk—oh let's get richard fucking burton in
altogether, shall we?—they say the welsh are thieves, don't
they?—at least in liverpool they do—count the silver once
richard burton's fucked off again—all this chatter—i mean,
really!—as I still can I will—boskier!—[indecipherable]—i'm
on my fucking island at last—close my fucking eyes—walk a
slow curve around that fucking egg—the giant egg shimmers and rocks a bit—soft throbs or thuds of life therein—
the past is about—the black skin of the water moves—i'm as
well to walk on—flower-brained and heron-eyed—just leave
me fucking be just leave me fucking be on my own fucking
island at last—at the bottom of the sea there are a million
tiny rooms but no doors no locks no keys—it's the past that
gets locked in—the sea is moving its inks about—close my
eyes as i walk i've gone inside the past again—slip inside the
old house then—uncle's come up the stairs—uncle travels
on a broken lung—wheezes like a busted accordion uncle
maudlin's travelling lung—the way his lips make the words
and the news they bring—she's gone, john—motherless
waif left on the docks or some such violin fucking thing—
she's gone—put a hole in my arm and let all the money in—a
rabid fast snare here? and building?—the stars hang down
like blue fruit—lovely?—the past is about—ye cracke is my
boozer it smells of dirty girls and beer—i am made of bile
and nerves and broken glass—i've got such a screechy, such
a girly laugh—the war room at ye cracke—keep it fucking

down, john—midnight by the churchbells—fucking some
girly in a doorway someplace—back arse of bold street—a
knee-trembler—the city is held in the palm of its own
lights—oh to be on an island by night—the birds home in
like rueful thoughts—thank you, charlie, it is nice—there's a
great lairy bird on patrol—don't give me the nazi fucking
eyes, pal—i'm the intruder on the stones and grass—there is
no salve and there is no fix—she is on the dark side of every
passing moment—this is my disease—she's a shadow just
beneath my skin—julia—and the island seems to move or
give in the night's black wind—[indecipherable]—let me go
back there, mr. haimes—close my eyes—the island by
night—the giant fucking egg groans—rouses from a sour
dream—there's a strange green light across the sky—green
as a starling's coat—iridescent—this is going fucking beautifully now—a sea-holly or an ivy's green—ivy as of a churchyard in november—the past is about—rain in liverpool, a
november, about the time of all souls, in the midweek, it's
late in the morning, i should be in the schoolhouse but i'm
not—i'm in a churchyard having a fag under the dripping
ivy—the way it's dull but glossy the way its own lights are
trapped within—i've got a throb on but one must not attend
to that in the out-of-doors as it sets a dangerous precedent—
next thing you know you're wanking off all over—there is
rain on the island by night—there is no way to mark time out
here but day for night and night for day again—the years
might go past—the rain tastes of salt and earth—the giant
fucking egg groans—who'll step out from that egg in a bit?—
i'm in on business i'm in on executive fucking business to
haunt the rooms of my own black self—the past is about—

over the ice fields of quebec we flew—four voices in a great dark hall—montreal—those sexy rascals—*lah-de-dah, lah-de-dum-dum-dah*—screams and mouths like black maws like the mouths of tiny birds to be fed—what if the giant fucking egg cracks and the past steps out?—i'd like five minutes back, not more—set me down on bold street—on the island the night crowds in and i scream but it gets swallowed up again—slap my head off this rock for a bit?—what if there's not much time left after this?—all the black chatter that goes on—walk awhile across the dark and stones of it—there are lights on the hills on the mainland—this exiled prince on scepter'd isle, handsome, beak-faced, and heron-thin—i'll have a fag in a bit—i am so many miles from love and home—the night birds shriek and grumble—the black water moves—where you lie down is the centre of my world, my love—i wanted to fuck you eleven ways and did—crossing the causeway is like crossing the moon—great boulders and stones and the black water moves—the starlight runs on cold engines—birds in conference the length of the night—a huge grey bird hides its head beneath its wing but fans it back slowly to show the evil eye as i pass—something regal, isn't there?—i'll have a sitdown—auntish moment—darling mimi—i lean back into the night sky—it's terrifying, of course, this fucking sentiment—so crucify me up top of fucking bold street then—sell fucking tickets—is there not such a thing as agency? my sweet english fucking arse there isn't—there's maggots under the rock with more agency—there's pigeons up the town clock—but you can be for a while whoever you decide to be—that's all—where I walk is the centre of the fucking universe—this is what you must

always believe—have you got that, kids?—what did it feel
like in sefton park?—he's a gimp and she's a skittery a nervous a scattered young thing—did she call him alf or did she
call him freddie?—he's doing all the voices—the way she
fixes her hair—he wants to have in—she wants to let him
in—did he drop the hand first thing?—on lark lane i will
walk you home again—they are so far from me now and
gone—across the fields of the sea—it's harder to think about
him than her—the cold is deep in my blood and bones—
walk awhile under the dying stars—the morning comes
across the water—the giant fucking egg groans—the giant
fucking egg cracks—he climbs out in red raw skin and greasy
feathers—his blistered black beseeching eyes—alright, freddie? alright, kid?—he lies among the rocks in his feathers
and bones and cowers from me there—alfred?—his first war
face—and i have nothing left to say—lay my hand to his
face—he sighs a tiny breath onto my palm—he grows smaller
with each breath that I take—i have nothing left to say—take
me away from here—put me back on bold street—let me
walk the street in the crowd—the bombed-out church—the
starlings mobbed above the ropewalks—a fair-minded
breeze lifts the cup of a skirt and shows the back of her
knee—she is not a showstopper but still—bold street
moves—a mam and a dad and a sticky-faced kiddie—the
bawl of the child as it comes past—he's pig-ugly him, missus,
there's a case here for your coupons back—a weary widow on
a ritual traipse—it's all ahead of you, love—and a toppling
quiff above a dummkopf face—a whiskied old fart in his
green and piss-stained gaberdine twill—the lyceum—the
tunnel for central station—bold street—the chinless won-

ders and the gin-blossom noses—i might have a show coming soon—i might get to play out again soon—if it works out with mr. knowles in ecclesworth—who's a cunt—or mr. eccles in knowleston—fifteen bob and a root up the arse—the street moves—there are pale sisters by cripp's—they're having a bead at the girdles and the dainties—if i burn the eyes on hard she'll sense it and turn, the prettier one—she turns—alright?—perky noses, sisterly grins—bold street moves—the way the knit of her collarbone turns as she goes—a cat watches from the lyceum steps—all the calm of china in its bone-white eyes—the busy faces—the pug faces—the lancashire-irish—the eaves of the stores and the eaves of the churches—i'm by the fucking lyceum—i'm by the window of cripp's—i'm the natty cocksparrow—the turn for the tunnel for central station—the sisters again—they whisper and turn again—the prettier's hand is held over her mouth—her face is pale and interested—her hand is white and tiny—a glove of bird bones—i'm by the lyceum—i'm by the turn for the tunnel for central station—military click of high heels on the stones of bold street—the city rumbles beneath—its limestone air and secret reaches—the scent of the girls' voices is on the air—their voices are coloured yellow and racing green—their voices come from the hollows of the woods—by the steamy window of a murderous caff a gummy old coot commits an act of murder on a plate of black pudding and chips—hello, tony? hello, taff—i walk the street in the crowd—pub voices bounce from the tiles and brass—sexy cured tobacco voices—ladies of special vintage—the painted lips and map-lined faces—the bowl of the town fills up with night—out there is the green moving estuary—out there are the devil-haunted hills—the first stars light the cold estates—i'll make a nonsense rhyme for my dandy lips—*oh to be a suburban jack, fit for the mirror and fit for the rack*—the turn for central station—the white cat smiles—and listen?—the world is still this faraway evening, as hushed and hollow as an empty church, and we can be quiet now if we want to be.

Part Nine

THE CARNIVAL IS OVER

The island was fucking exhausting. He didn't last for long out there. Now he waits it out at the farmhouse in the hills. Soon the car will come to bring him to the airport—Cornelius—and soon he will be in the sky again. He sits in a hard chair by the webby kitchen window—in the webs he sees a languid man. He has the place to himself and the day is not without its graces: a duck walks across a puddle in the yard. Appears to be on very serious business. A dog is yowling somewhere far off. They might never think to find me in these demented reaches. He drinks strong tea and smokes a fag—stay fucking busy, John. Bridge off all the silences and the gaps.

Soon he will be able to make something new. He will make something delicate and fine and odd. It's all going to work out beautifully. Because he is our fucking hero still. He can see down the hills and to the water. Time slows just enough for its workings to show—just oddly, here and there, as it will do in the Maytime. The moments bead into each other, one by one and neatly, but sometimes they reverse and spin back, too, and this explains plenty. It turns out you can play with it a bit. You can make time spin back towards you. He breathes deep and feels out the serpent length of himself. A vitamin sadness fills his lungs. Where might I get to if I persist with all this? Getting fucking Saviour notions again. He can see the tiny details and he can see the broader sweep. There is rain now on the roof slates and a concertina wind. The Irish coast sits down there in its drizzle and murk. You wouldn't know where the fuck you are nor when.

———

He walks for a while in the hills above Mulranny. It is very quiet. He walks by the old railway line. Now it has cleared and the day is lit. There are no people anywhere to be seen. Shades of the railway line move at an unseen thrum. He sits and rests for a while in a scooped-out hollow of the hillside. The breeze snaps and dies and there is perfect quiet across the sky and blue of bay. Something moves. He sits as still as he can and dares hardly to breathe. In the far left field of his vision if he does not move at all maybe the hare will not disappear. He read once that the hare augurs darkly in the Irish mythology. From what he can remember there is fuck all that augurs brightly in the Irish mythology. The hare is no more than a couple of yards away. It is so close he can see reflected in its startled eye the grey stone of hill and blue of bay. It looks out across the flank of the hill but it cannot see him in the hollow. Its nose is a soft purse leather and it twitches to find the strangeness on the air but it cannot place him. Do you not hear my heart racing? A crack of the breeze snaps the tall grasses—everything is immense. He sits perfectly still and grins madly—he is nothing but the grin. The hare rises on its hind legs—it stands mannishly.

Actually quite a handsome devil. It is poised in every twitch and sinew to run but still there is this strangeness on the air it cannot twig. Oh Jesus fuck let this moment hold across the sky and blue of bay. The hare turns its nose a tiny mechanical clockwork nidge. It surveys the fields of the Maytime in the hills above Mulranny. From the hotel far below comes a sudden clanging—the kitchens—and the hare takes off as quick as light moves and its pumping run sounds out the hollows of the hill. Fuck me. He gets up and walks for a while again. He goes on down the beach and has a fag. There are further Victorians on the beach. He calls a salute to them as he passes by—

Alright?

—but they just shyly, stiffly wave.

———

Back in the farmhouse.

Cornelius enters, red-faced, and in a fluster—

This is not a happy day for the Mercedes, John.

Oh?

Exhaust is crooked on it again. There's a man in Mulranny might fix it and drop it up to us tonight but he is not a reliable man and he suffers from fainting fits.

I see.

The worse news is I think the van's on the way out as well.

Tea is made. They wait on the man from Mulranny. There is dangerous talk of black pudding sandwiches.

———

He paces the yard. He thinks about what to say to his love, exactly, and he thinks about holding the kid. He has a fag to batten down the emotional bits. He leans back against the wall of the farmhouse high in County Mayo and the Atlantic rolls down there—a Mesmeric—and if you close your eyes you can fall into its black drift and turn and you can be wherever you want to be.

———

On Bold Street he walks the street in the crowd. He wears a drape jacket in midnight green with a velvet collar of dark cherry, or call it cerise, and high-waisted drainpipes in a navy-black mottle cut an inch above the ankle to show leopard-print socks and crêpe-sole brothel creepers in a desert-brown and most delicate suede and his hair is greased and fixed to hold on a ducktail finish and the curl of his lip spells seventeen and he's that fucking sharp except he's got his mum beside. A tadpole kid passes by on a rusty bike. The kid jerks a foot to the kerb and turns the bike sideways to block the path. He looks hard at John. He says—

I heard there was a nigger boat done over.

She goes right up close to the kid. She fronts him. The way she stands there, stone hard, and says—

Fuck off.

And the kid fucks off.

———

The man from Mulranny does not appear.

Do you see now the way I'm half my life down the far end of lanes waiting on thundering bastards who don't show up, John?

Well this is it.

The van also has given its last.

We'll take it by foot, John. We'll find out what's happening with the Mercedes at least.

They walk down the mountain. They are headed for Mulranny. They walk the country by night. They come to the water and follow the long, dark, turning sea road. The world tonight is a monochrome dream. A pockfaced moon browses the road and bay. Cornelius raises his glance to curse it—

Fucken thing, he says.

There is an odd drag from it.

As long as we're not steered by it, John.

The birds of the night chorus in a hedgerow like fat young lawyers—a prosperous choir. Onwards—this sentimental journey. One honky step in front of the other. Now the road comes up as though on a riser and the sea opens out above the rocks and a swarm of moving lights passes through the water—a shoal?

Precisely so, Cornelius says.

It electrifies, but the road turns again as quickly inland to the dark stone empire and the hills of the night. There is a figure up ahead, a shade.

Fuck me, he says.

Now, says Cornelius. This particular lady, John?

Yes?

A hundred and twelve years of age and hoppin' off the road.

Okay.

———

Good evening, Margaret?

Cornelius, she says, and does not turn her eyes at all.

This is Kenneth, Margaret, a cousin of mine home from England.

How are you, Ken, she says, and does not turn her eyes at all.

I'm not bad—she turns at his voice.

Right, she says.

Margaret, tell us this, because he won't believe me. What age have you now?

I've a hundred and twelve years of age, she says.

And how does that feel? John says.

Rough, she says.

Do the maths for us, Margaret.

I was born, she says, in 1866.

They were jawin' grass at the side of the road, Ken.

Fuck me.

But Margaret will not be caught on memory—ask her anything you like.

What kind of thing?

Anything at all, watch—Margaret, on what account was the 1943 Munster Final cancelled?

On account of an outbreak of foot and mouth disease.

Do you see that, Ken?

She wears a pink raincoat to her ankles and a pair of high yellow Adidas runners. What's left of hair in scrags is dyed a glossy black—like scraps of feathers dipped in oil and twisted.

She looks at John with interest now.

Have you been on the television?

Maybe I have.

When you were younger, she says.

Well this is it.

I'd recognise the nose, she says. You've a bit of weight gone off you since?

I've gone macrobiotic now.

There were four of ye, she says.

There were.

The leader was a beautiful-looking boy, she says. The big eyes like saucers and the song about the blackbird.

Okay, John says.

Now, Margaret, Cornelius says. If a young man like this was looking for answers about his feelings, what kind of thing would you tell him?

What class of feelings is he having?

Very fucking complicated ones, John says.

I'll tell you one thing you could do, she says. You could put a clean tongue inside your mouth.

I'm sorry.

Anyway, she says, and she looks out to the sea again and shakes her head sadly. The best thing is not to feel at all. It's all hell after fifty, boys.

She turns to him a last time—

But no harm sometimes to have that bit of arrogance in yourself.

———

The examined life turns out to be a pain in the stones. The only escape from yourself is to scream and fuck and make and do. He will not go back any more to the old places. He will not go back to Sefton Park.

—————

He stepped out from the shade of a tree. He was blinded in the sun. He wore a stupid bowler hat. He came across looking kind of sulphurous. He sat beside her on the bench. What do you think of my hat, he said. It's stupid, she said, and he took it off and threw it in the duck pond. The way that her heart vaulted its beat.

These are dangerous words on our lips, Freddie.

It was in the Trocadero she saw him first. There was something in his voice that made a scratch come into hers when she spoke. She told him not to touch so much and he got a face on like a washed dog.

He wanted to fish his hat from the pond again but could not reach. The way that he stood there with his hands on his skinny girlish hips.

You could have a paddle, she said.

It was cold in the park in the springtime in the sunshine. He rubbered his lips and clowned his love for her—she might kiss him if he tried it—and he wiped his hands off the seat of his shiny pants as though to say this is all settled and now there are two of us in it, Julia.

———

The black swarm of the sea moves its lights like a cocaine palace.

I beg your pardon, John?

It's a lyric, Cornelius. Or at least a note towards one. I'm thinking it all through.

I have you.

I just let the words come out, really, in just a sort of ... *blaaaah*. You know, without thinking? In just a kind of ... *bleuurrgh*. Without thinking. To get the subconscious stuff? And then I see if I can get a shape on them.

Is that how it works?

Sometimes. But the imagination is a very weak little bird. It flounders, Cornelius, and it flaps about a bit.

I'd believe it, John. Cocaine I never took.

I'm inclined to think that's a very good idea.

Though I was addicted to cough bottles at one time.

Tell me more.

I was drinking five or six of them a night after my supper.

Jesus Christ. What does six cough bottles down the hatch feel like?

Like an eiderdown wrapped around yourself. It feels like goose feathers. It feels like mother's love. No matter how hard or cruel the world or the night might be you're . . . like a baby . . . kind of . . . What's the word I'm after, John?

Swaddled?

Is right. Against all the harshness of the world.

Were there hallucinations, Cornelius?

Were there fucken what. I had a very firm belief—this went on for months unending—that a particular gap in the hill on the road towards the Highwood was a kind of wink at me, in the night, as I drove through. As if the mountain was marking the passage of time for me in a sort of cheeky way.

The gap in the hill was a wink?

Just so. In the headlights as I drove through.

Cornelius?

John?

Oh nothing.

———

They come to Mulranny. A small bar with a low peat fire is chosen for discretion's need. He orders a pot of tea only but large ham-faced gentlemen with farmer hands and farm demeanour appear at frequent intervals and freshen the pot with small measures of whiskey. In what seems like no time at all there is interested talk of the Highwood. Certainly we wouldn't be kept late, Ken, there is no music tonight or at least there is no music that is scheduled. Complicated phone calls are made about motor vehicles. A consensus arrives that to be relaxed about things is the best policy as all told we are unlikely to be found wanting for a vehicle. Of course it's the same attitude has this country on its fucken knees but even so. The only question really is where we are headed for and that is a question that opens out to life generally and is as well ignored. There are planes across the sky and ocean every day of the week is the truth of it. The dog Brian Wilson puts in an appearance, shuffling through the doors a little sheepishly, like a regular lately barred from the place. He takes his ease by the fire. He is accompanied by his charge, a fluttering person with an oblong head who is known as Dutch Mike. I've met this dog in Newport town, you know? When was this? Quite early one recent morning. Newport . . . is that where he goes? Yes, and he has quite a nice singing voice. The night opens out to itself not unreasonably. People come, people go, and a ride is arranged for the Highwood. The stars are out to travel the road above us gaily. Kenneth is an accepted oddity of the western hills now or at least this is how we will allow it to appear. And there is magic, isn't there, in the way the Maytime opens out to us?

———

It comes along to the morning again. He walks the broad deserted beach at Mulranny. It is bright and cold and his blood tingles with news. He is in a state of relief that cannot be put into words because it is internal and of the blood. The breeze has sharp cold points and he huddles against it in the old man's suit as he walks. Ambles—the word appears on his lips unasked for and he laughs at it. I'll have an amble for a bit. The sand circles in small drifts and patters brightly and sighs when it falls to settle in the breezeless gaps. Tiny comic birds run on spindle legs from the foaming waves and put up their outraged chatter. A disbelieving crow watches in jackboots and makes a depressed cawing. There is the fall of his own step and the easy labour of his breathing and now across the sand a black bead hovers in the distance moving and it comes closer and rises to a low contented humming above the sound of the birds and his breath and his step falling and as it approaches—the old Mercedes—it slows with nice decorum and the back door falls open for him.

———

The tadpole kid's bike creaks on its rusted chain as he takes off again and we walk together down Bold Street in the afternoon and though I can see your lips move and I can hear your voice still I cannot make out the words anymore but for the single word—John—and it's a routine traipse or escapade, Wednesdayish, to a bun shop or a caff or the music shop to pay off an instalment, maybe, and I can see you as you turn to me and laugh and we're by the turn for the tunnel for Central station and I cannot make out the words anymore and this is very hard to do because love is so very hard to do. But I can see you on Bold Street as we move with the crowd again and there is a catch or snag in your voice—a scratch, a sadness—that tells me the way that time moves and summer soon across the trees will spin its green strands.